Andrew Cotto

Cucina Romana

Another Italian Adventure

A Novel

Black Rose Writing | Texas

ISBN: 978-1-68433-669-2
PUBLISHED BY BLACK ROSE WRITING
www.blackrosewriting.com

Printed in the United States of America
Suggested Retail Price (SRP) $18.95

Cucina Romana is printed in Georgia

*As a planet-friendly publisher, Black Rose Writing does its best to eliminate unnecessary waste to reduce paper usage and energy costs, while never compromising the reading experience. As a result, the final word count vs. page count may not meet common expectations.

To my children, Sophia and Julian, who I hope will inherit their father's love of Italy and the pleasures of being around the table.

Cucina Romana

Another Italian Adventure

Chapter 1

Jacoby Pines opened his eyes in the hills south of Florence, in the light-filled loft of a renovated barn beside a villa. It was where he lived. And this reality still started each morning with a jolt of wonder and a flash of doubt, even though it had been months since he arrived in Italy on holiday with his former fiancée, and only weeks after that when his fortunes dramatically changed. Over the course of those initial days, and on one most miraculous afternoon, something happened that would insure his remaining in Italy as long as he wished, which was forever.

It was the day his fate had been delivered to him, whether by destiny or serendipity, it did not matter. Jacoby, no longer engaged to be married but romantically involved with someone else, now co-owned a hotel in the quaintest of Tuscan villages, mere miles from Florence proper yet unfettered by tourists. The hotel once belonged to ancestors he knew nothing of, beyond an anonymous photograph from the middle of the previous century that clandestinely accompanied him to Italy and provided some hope in a life which was, to that point, devoid of blessings. And his co-owner in the hotel, an expat septuagenarian from Texas named Bill Guion, had fast become the closest friend Jacoby had had in his 32 years of an itinerant and often lonely campaign. He also had a dog in Italy named "Boy." A spotted Australian border collie who slept at Jacoby's side each night and jumped up from bed with him every morning.

The wooden doors to the Juliet balcony were open, and the thin curtains billowed in a breeze that carried rosemary and sage to Jacoby's olfactory acuteness. The parted curtains revealed the olive trees, shimmering slate-green leaves dappled in fledgling sunshine, in a grove that rose toward the ridge offering a spectacular view of Florence. Jacoby and Boy visited the overlook nearly every morning as both a ritual and a reminder of the abundant splendor available in Italy. It also reminded Jacoby that he was in love, for the first time in his life, with a place.

After the dramatic events of the previous June, the summer had been spent adjusting to the reality that his entire orbit had been turned on its axis, and that dreams coming true can be as hard to accept as great misfortune. Jacoby, a few celebratory days after it all went down, sensed a need of reconciliation, of adjustment through prosaic efforts. He spent the summer in simplicity, not doing much beyond living the way his new Italian friends and neighbors lived, afraid to venture too far from his routine and surroundings for fear that it all might disappear.

Down the spiral staircase to the lower-level of the barn, Jacoby took a large glass of water in the kitchenette and filled Boy's ceramic bowl. They drank and then crossed through the muted, cool living area with a floor of ancient tiles and a ceiling of exposed beams. There was a small sofa, a round, wooden table and an antique credenza that contained Jacoby's modest wine collection. The only other room on the ground floor was adjacent to the staircase, full of natural light, with an antique desk and a leather sofa where Jacoby read books or played guitar.

The guitar was a gift from Giovanni, the young, artisan cobbler in town whom Jacoby had accompanied in a cover gig during the village's recent festival. Both the festival and the gig ended in a brawl with Jacoby breaking his previous guitar over the back of a malevolent hunter. The hunter was once the master of Boy and was still the husband, albeit estranged, of Giovanni's love, Nicoletta.

The events still struck Jacoby as fantastic, and he couldn't help but grin at the whole affair as he parted the swinging doors that sealed the barn's lower level from light. He opened the antique, windowed partition which would remain the only barrier to entry until he sealed the swinging doors before bed.

The terracotta terrace, covered in morning dew, was cool even through shoes, and the rosemary hedge that draped the stone wall buzzed with insects. Beyond the high fence was the villa where Jacoby's landlord, Paolo, lived alone and kept mostly to himself.

"Come on, Boy," Jacoby called the dog as he sniffed after a buzzing bee.

Boy followed Jacoby up the curved stairway of stone, under the sagging branches of a fig tree heavy with fruit, a few of which Jacoby collected, and into the olive grove of gnarled trunks and taut branches shimmering with slate-green leaves. The base of the trees were surrounded by nets that Paolo used to collect the dark olives ready for harvest. The whole area - as all of Tuscany and all of Italy - was in the initial throes of the harvest season, where the most precious products of this blessed peninsula were gathered at their peak and converted into oil and wine.

The days in the heart of autumn were long and full of light. Jacoby did not want them to end, especially as he, someone who knew isolation and depression, was dreading the rainy season that followed. But there was so much to look forward to before then, so much to do to stay busy and enjoy the miracle that had become his life: the acquisition and reopening of the hotel, the oversight of the renovation of his family's former estate (now owned by his former-fiancée's outrageous cousin, Dolores) and the village's harvest celebration that would, if as planned, mark the debut of the repurposed hotel.

And, of course, there was the everyday beauty - of food and wine and topography - that Jacoby cherished along with his new friends and his new community and this dog named Boy who padded alongside Jacoby as they approached the ridge where below, bathed in lemon-tinged light, lie the city of Florence: a spooned circle of terracotta and stone and pastels, split horizontally by the nearby River Arno and surrounded by verdant hills like a lush hood framing the face of a movie star. It still seemed, after all these looks, like a model, a tiny replica of plastic pieces, of a make believe place, not a real place in real size made by the hands of men many centuries ago. A city of domes and towers and palaces, of serpentine streets and quaint lanes, of four bridges that spanned the Arno, including the famous Ponte Vecchio, lined with jewelry shops of pastel facades.

And making Florence, and everything else, all the more fantastic was that Helen Dempsey lived down there, above a shop in a tiny piazza in the Santo Spirito quarter on the less-traversed side of the Arno. Helen had accompanied Jacoby and Bill during the wildest night of their Italian adventure and then, on a separate occasion, presented Jacoby the most romantic day he had ever known.

When he had left Helen's apartment the next morning, he was within a few days of his undesired return to America, defeated yet determined to return to Italy at some point, to surprise Helen near the Uffizi Galleria where she spent her days as a museum guide explaining the magnificent collection of Italian art to English-speaking tourists who surely found her as adorable and mesmerizing as Jacoby did.

He assured Helen of his return, although it might be years. Instead, he never left and returned to find Helen in a matter of days. And Jacoby waited nervously for her to finish work, sitting in the same gazebo, out front of a hotel, in the Piazza della Signoria near the Uffizi, where the two had first met over a glass of prosecco. The fading light gathered in the sky above the piazza's roof line; shadows cloaked the facades and statues and fountains; the elegant residents in their tailored clothes passed during their evening walk, and Jacoby squeezed the slippery stem of a flute full of prosecco, filled from a bottle plunged in ice aside an empty glass on a table for two, rehearsing his charming line, which he failed to mutter as Helen eventually flitted past on her bicycle.

"Hey!" he called, desperate and loud, before Helen could peddle out of sight.

The whole piazza seemed to stop, as Italians - especially in this well-heeled part of town - simply did not yell. Shame swarmed Jacoby's forehead and sweat broke out across his shoulders. He felt like an ugly American, the very image he was most eager to avoid. Helen skidded to a stop and tilted her chin toward the outburst.

"My, my, Jacoby Pines," she said. "What took you so long?"

Jacoby's cavity filled with a feeling of warmth that reminded him, for the first time, of the long, lost love he had for his mother who had died when he was just a boy. Jacoby put the glass of prosecco down and climbed over the gazebo's railing to cross the piazza with his eyes locked on Helen, who stood holding her bike until Jacoby neared and she let it fall to the ground. They grasped each other by the torsos and held each other without moving as darkness sifted down and the citizens of Florence passed the flesh and blood couple, aside a fallen bicycle, who rivaled the magnificent statues that filled the glorious piazza.

Helen's tears moistened the fine linen shirt Jacoby had purchased for the occasion. Abruptly, she pushed him away and bumped him once hard on the chest. "I've missed you, you know?"

"I missed you, too," he said, the words cracking in his throat as his head spun from emotional deliverance.

She looked around the piazza, trying to gather her senses, and her sense of logic. "But what are you doing here? Why are you back? Did you ever leave?"

Jacoby picked up Helen's bike and led her by the hand back to the gazebo, where they sat in the magical light at a table for two, and Jacoby explained what had transpired since he left her apartment a few days prior. Helen gasped and giggled and went through three glasses of prosecco before Jacoby had finished the fantastic story of how the village festival was a massive success—particularly the cinghiale ragu Bill had prepared from the beast Jacoby had slayed with an ax—until hubris got the best of Giovanni during their short concert of Pearl Jam covers, causing a brawl to break out between the two musicians and a gang of hunters.

"Well," Helen said, contradicting a line she had once used to describe Jacoby's plight. "You no longer seem like your very own lost generation."

Jacoby smiled and sipped prosecco. "I am so found," he said.

"But how does that explain why you are here now?"

"This is the best part..." he continued on about how the next day, the very day he was supposed to return to America, and the day his bankrupt ancestor's estate was to be auctioned, fate arrived in news of a wrongful termination settlement regarding his firing in New York. He was redeemed. And wealthy. Jacoby suddenly had enough money to not just stay in Italy but partner with Bill in the purchase of the hotel in the village, while the enormously wealthy English cousin of his former-fiancée purchased the massive villa in the countryside and its auspices for wine and olive oil production, a property which she - based in London - asked Jacoby to look after in its rehabilitation into a resort, and to manage upon completion.

"That's almost too fantastic for words," Helen said.

"I know," he said. "I know."

And Jacoby remembered his miraculous story as he looked over Florence each morning and thought of Helen and the recent events that had reshaped his life, eating fresh figs and petting his dog as the sun rose on yet another beautiful day in the most beautiful place in all of the world.

Chapter 2

The walk to the village began with the bumpy access road of dirt and stone, bordered by an Etruscan wall on one side and a verdant valley sown with wild grass and poppies and sunflowers on the other. The Spanish-tiled roofs of distanced villas appeared in the dancing morning light, beyond the tops of umbrella pines and cypress trees. A wide, solid fence had been installed at the bottom of the road, where it met the paved track that curved down from the hills into the ramparts of Florence proper. The fence was built to keep out the hunters who illegally stalked the elevated and wooded surroundings in search of cinghiale and their desired edible of black truffles. Paolo and his neighbors had arranged for the fence after the brawl in the village piazza, certain that the malevolent hunters would be even more defiant than before.

Jacoby was particularly pleased with the fence, being one of the hunters' primary adversaries and the new master of their leader's dog. It was their trespassing that had familiarized Boy with the area where Jacoby lived and how he ended up under Jacoby's care after being saved from the tusks of a massive cinghiale by a single swing of an ax. And it was also that courageous act that had made Jacoby a hero in the village as the story of the felled boar became an instant legend and the meat of the delicacy provided a ragu for the village sagra. The strange American with the strange name became "Jake, il americano." And this legend status only increased with the brawl at the end of the sagra where Jacoby and Giovanni, in front of most of the village, fought off five hunters in dramatic fashion and then partied like rock stars.

And as much as Jacoby had no regrets about any of the events which led to his new status as a fledgling ex-pat, concern about the hunters and their eventual return crept around the fortress walls of his mind, especially as he descended from the hills each morning, Boy at this side, on the dirt track through the olive groves, watching for serpents and breathing deep the fragrant air, before joining the two-lane road and turning the hairpin and narrow bend that fed into the village piazza.

The rectangular space, surrounded by low-slung facades of sandstone and pastel, held all of life's necessities: butcher shop, fruit & vegetable stand, news kiosk, bottega, gelato shop, tailor, wine consortium, barber, housewares, gift shop, shoe store. Just beyond the piazza was a bakery, a small supermarket, and an open area where a market was held twice a week that featured fashionable garments from Florence, a fishmonger from the Tyrrhenian coast and a rotisserie stand run by farmers from the Tuscan hills. Back in the piazza, of course, was also the hotel Jacoby owned with Bill, where he would report each morning after taking a coffee and pastry from the well-lit and airy cafe on the piazza's far corner.

"Buongiorno, Nicoletta," Jacoby said.

"Ciao, americano," she responded with her familiar, wan smile before coming from behind the bar to praise and pet the dog once treated so indifferently by her estranged husband.

She had offered the dog to Jacoby after he had saved it from the beast, but Jacoby refused, citing, at the time, his imminent return to America. Of all the moments of those painful days, that was the most excruciating, since it lay bare the hard reality that he had no home for himself nor a dog, not in Italy and not in America. He had never felt so displaced.

But Jacoby's post-salvation days were highlighted by the arrival of Nicoletta and Giovanni outside the gate of Paolo's villa, the clandestine couple now public with their love, calling for "Jake! Jake! Jake!" Jacoby hurried outside, to open the mechanical fence with a remote, happy to be called on by new friends only to find with the swinging gate a charging border collie and Nicoletta and Giovanni waving goodbye.

The memory was among the many of late that Jacoby kept like feathers tucked into the cap of his heart. And his heart bound, like his loving new dog, each morning upon entering the cafe to greet his friend and take his coffee and a small pastry, just one of the simple pleasures in a place of such plenty.

Jacoby took extra solace each morning when the parking spot aside the cafe was not inhabited by the hunter's jeep, though he knew it would return at some point. He dashed this thought, as he routinely did, leaving the cafe to cross the piazza, past the statue of the village founder, as morning doves cooed from the eves and pigeons pecked around the stone surface, and the sun rose above the hills as the piazza shops began to open. The hotel was catty-cornered from the cafe, two buildings down from the newsstand and barbershop. It was of faded sandstone with an ornate set of front doors where a modest bronze plaque read: Hotel Floria-Zanobini.

Jacoby learned that was his family's name: Floria-Zanobini. It was surely more impressive than his actual family name: Pines. And he also learned, during his recent adventure, the name of his Italian ancestors extended back to the Roman empire and included his mother, the granddaughter of the Floria-Zanobini heiress who fell in love with an American soldier during World War II and abandoned her family, and her once-prestigious ancestry, for America. This escape was so thorough that it was never spoken of until Jacoby arrived from America with a photograph and a desperation to find his ancestors.

Jacoby had no idea about the photograph's importance. He knew nothing of his family and almost nothing even of his mother who had died so long ago. His only memory of her was olfactory, the faint smell of baking cookies emitted from a factory located near the park where his mother would take him to play as a toddler. His father did not speak of her, and Jacoby assumed during their itinerant and often lonely life together that his father's perpetual melancholy was the product of a broken heart, so he did not pry. A consideration of his mother only returned after his father's passing when he found a box of her belongings that included a faded photograph of a lovely woman with an elegant dress furled below her on the lawn of a grand estate. The back of the photo read: Villa Floria-Zanobini 1939.

And this photo secretly accompanied Jacoby to Italy where he was supposed to live for a year with his travel-writer fiancée and recover from his defeat in America, before returning to redeem himself in the professional ranks of New York City. The photograph's unknown origins actually fueled his belief in fate, his fantastic notion of finding a long-lost family in Italy and staying there forever. And even though this fantasy didn't actually come to fruition as imagined, as there was no family left, Jacoby's pursuit of heritage did deliver his dream, and, as a tertiary benefit, he felt connected to his mother like never before, his thoughts of her more frequent and vivid and not solely prompted by the smell of baking cookies but by myriad aspects of Italy, as if even the sun on his face spoke of her. It was as if she were still alive.

He especially thought of his mother each morning as he entered the hotel and touched the plaque on the door that recognized her family's name.

Chapter 3

The hotel lobby was cool and shaded, a small welcome area with space rugs over marble floors, a comfortable couch and some chairs, a desk in the open with a computer, a bookshelf covering one wall and paintings of the Italian countryside on the others. It was all very functional, maintained by Bill for years as simply a place where connections to the family stayed on their way through Tuscany. More of a fancy hostel than a hotel, but that was going to change. And soon.

The issue wasn't updating the property, as it was with the enormous estate in the countryside which Jacoby was overseeing on behalf of Dolores. The eight guest rooms of the hotel, along with the dining area and the back terrace, were all in the same pristine condition as the lobby. The Hotel Floria-Zanobini, and the village of Antella where it was located, both suffered from anonymity. No one outside of the immediate auspices had heard of either. Antella appeared, albeit in limited scope, in Google searches; the hotel did not.

Jacoby spent his mornings at the desktop in the lobby trying to change that. He had worked in PR back in New York, in the music industry, not travel, but he knew how to drum up publicity by contacting publications and freelance writers. He already had a win, a solid bit of press coming from Claire, his travel writing ex-fiancée who shared a story on the hotel with *Off the Gilded Path*, the new travel site of the world-renowned Haxby's Guide. Jacoby had jokingly referred to the new media venture as "Four-Star Slumming" which was exactly what the hotel was offering in comfortable luxury as opposed to opulence and in locations decidedly unfettered by tourism. The article and any that followed would have to wait until the paperwork with regard to the transfer of ownership was formalized, a task all the more complicated by the fact that neither Jacoby nor Bill were Italian citizens. This convoluted pursuit was how Bill spent his days, making cell phone calls to local officials in Florence and government offices in Rome. Battling Italian bureaucracy, Jacoby recognized, was a far more difficult endeavor than currying favor with English-speaking travel writers eager for stories about Italy.

The partners met each weekday for a mid-morning cappuccino that Bill prepared in the hotel's pristine kitchen. The frothy cups were taken in the light-filled dining area or the adjacent courtyard out back. The conversations were similar each day, updates from Jacoby on publicity pursuits and complaints from Bill about Italian inefficiency. Jacoby could see the fatigue on Bill, his face more ruddy, his insouciant blue eyes less so, his step slower. Bill no longer rose early to forage along the roadside or in the woods. As of late, he'd been sleeping in his quarters upstairs right up until it was time to make the cappuccinos.

"So good," Jacoby said, as he did every morning with his first sip, the aroma filling his nose as the foam coated his upper lip, which he would pause to enjoy for a moment before licking it off.

Bill nodded cordially in his gentle way.

They were in the courtyard, at a wrought iron table with matching chairs under a trellis strung with wisteria vines. A garden with marked plots extended beyond the slate surface of the terrace. This was where Jacoby and Bill had had their first conversation many months before, where their Italian adventure was born, the morning Jacoby came to the village with the secret photograph, which led him to Bill who had a far more immediate connection to the image than Jacoby, even though the woman in the photo - unbeknownst to him at the time - was his grandmother.

The woman in the photograph had a brother named Filippo. He and Bill had been lovers for many decades. They met as journalists in Rome's AP bureau and lived together in romantic and cultural bliss in the Trastevere section of the city, where Bill transitioned into a career as a caterer, occasional instructor and private chef for an American university in the area, before the couple returned to Filippo's family estate in Florence to semi-retire as co-managers of the family's hotel.

Their modest plans were adversely affected by the family's matriarch, Filippo's mother, who rejected her son's homosexuality upon his return to Florence, though it had been openly acknowledged since his youth, severing ties with both him and the hotel in Antella. And then Filippo was diagnosed with stage 4 Pancreatic cancer, and any remaining plans died with him. Bill was left to run the hotel using a small stipend that arrived each month; his own savings, being an illegal immigrant, were in Filippo's accounts, which his mother seized upon the death of her son.

The theory among the villagers was that the reclusive matriarch of the Floria-Zanobini family had never emotionally recovered from the disappearance of her daughter during World War II, and that in her very old age she had spiraled into madness and dementia, rejecting her own son and last living relative. The photograph Jacoby had brought from America offered the first news of the matriarch's daughter and perhaps a reconciliation of sorts for Bill as well as a familial connection for Jacoby.

Unfortunately for Bill and Jacoby, the matriarch, at over 100 years old, had gone into hiding, and was only found upon her death bed where she was happy to learn of her daughter's happiness in America. She arranged for the return of Bill's savings, but was sad to report that the family estate was in bankruptcy and in the hands of the Italian government. It was then, in a moment of seeming despair where all hope was lost, that Jacoby's belief in fate was delivered, on the day he was to return to America, in the form of his wrongful termination settlement.

The wonder of these events, though, began to worry Jacoby. Perhaps immersing in such an endeavor was taking a toll on Bill. His new aura reminded Jacoby of his perpetually melancholy father who also suffered from a staggering heartbreak that he could not shake, something Jacoby believed led to his slow death some 30 years after. Jacoby could not imagine and could not witness Bill experiencing the same type of fatal and elongated march to death.

"Why don't we hire someone to handle all the legal rigmarole?" Jacoby suggested, nearly finished with his cappuccino, remnants of mocha-tinted foam gathering in the bottom of the cup.

Bill sighed and rubbed his trim, grey beard. "I'm afraid hiring someone would probably take too long and certainly be exorbitant in price."

"Let's just slow down then, go with the Italian pace and let things happen when they happen. You can do other things, work on the menu and maybe take a vacation somewhere."

"No. No," Bill said. "It's important we launch in conjunction with the harvest for reasons symbolic and financial. Unlike you, my dear boy, my finances are not infinite nor is my time on earth."

"I'm going to live forever?" Jacoby joked, sitting up straight.

Bill smiled. "I'm sorry, Jacoby. I'm a little on edge these days."

"I know," Jacoby pleaded, leaning forward, over the table, toward his friend. "That's why I say we take it easy. We can open in the spring. I'd love for you to go on a little vacation. Or a big vacation."

Bill pulled his flip phone out and put it face down on the table. He looked at the streaks of blue sky between the wisteria vines. "I've got a better idea," he said looking at Jacoby.

"What's that?"

"Let's go to Rome."

"Rome? Both of us?"

"Yes, I'd like you to come along, for reasons professional and perhaps personal as well. And you can't be in Italy and not see Rome," he said. "I haven't been since Filippo and I moved up here, and something is telling me that it's time for a visit. That something awaits."

Jacoby shrugged in agreement and tried to imagine what Rome would be like as he hadn't thought of Italy much beyond his immediate auspices in the hills south of Florence, the city itself, and Tuscany at large. He was becoming provincial, and he liked that. Bill cleared his throat to draw Jacoby's attention.

"And this is where you would, if on cue, offer your quote from Dante about fate."

Jacoby smiled an apology and recalled the time in Piazza di Santa Croce with Bill, in front of the towering statue of Dante Alighieri, when his own future was so in doubt, that he recited these lines of assurance from the Florentine poet, as he did once again, sitting with a forlorn Bill on the back terrace of their shared hotel: "Do not be afraid; our fate cannot be taken from us; it is a gift."

"Bravo," Bill said and nodded.

Jacoby nodded back. "So, what's the plan?"

"It will serve two purposes," Bill said. "Of a vacation, of sorts, an inaugural visit for you and one of reminiscence for me, but also business as we can call on the offices that I've had such a hard time getting assistance from by phone."

"Really? Would that work?"

"They can't put you on hold or simply not answer when you are standing there in person," Bill said with a coy look. "And beyond that, I could show you around bella Roma, the eternal city and the place where I left my heart."

"Works for me," Jacoby confirmed. "When do we leave?"

"How about tomorrow?"

Chapter 4

Boy, who was not allowed in the hotel per Bill's insistence and allergies, spent the morning around the cafe being spoiled and fed and hydrated by Nicoletta or frolicking alone in the woods. But when Jacoby left the hotel for lunch, the dog was waiting right outside the door, on his front haunches, eager to be with his new master each day at this time. Jacoby loved the unrelenting and unwavering love of his new dog and wished he had had one growing up. Maybe then he would not have been so lonely.

"Hi, Boy," Jacoby said kneeling down to pet the head and neck of his dog, whose tail wagged wildly, until it was time to secure some food.

The open air market was active that day, and Jacoby took from the rotisseria stand, in a cone of butcher's paper barely spotted with grease, some lightly-fried rabbit adorned in salt and rosemary and lemon. He crossed, with Boy at his heels, the piazza to the cafe where he sat at a small metal table, askance to the entrance in the space where the village children often played soccer after school.

Nicoletta came out of the cafe with a plate and cutlery for Jacoby, which she set up before returning with a glass of sparkling water and a small carafe of white wine. Jacoby carefully lay the cone across the plate, like a bouquet of his favorite flowers, and breathed in the savory, slightly astringent smell of the tender meat sealed in a crusted batter. Jacoby liked the way Italians fried things lightly, and he enjoyed the gentle crunch of the exterior and the seasonings it held before connecting with the toothy texture of the meat, which tasted of the grass and herbs and vegetables the animal now being consumed had once lived upon. The local white was made from Trebbiano grapes, and Jacoby preferred it very cold to temper the forward flavors of fruits and flowers.

After lunch, Jacoby would often take Boy for a walk beyond the piazza, across the village's public park and into the low-slung residential areas where the locals lived in modest apartments or co-joined homes of faded pastel facades, past old men smoking cigarettes and chatting on benches, housewives in housecoats in the midst of their daily chores. All would stop what they were doing to greet Jacoby with enthusiastic calls of "Ciao, Jake." Jacoby still basked in the popularity he enjoyed as not only an American in their midst but one who had killed a monstrous cinghiale with an ax and fought off the village brutes in a tremendous display of honor. They also, he believed, recognized his kindness and great happiness at being there. For many, he was the only person from outside the village they had ever met, and the fact that he, a young and appealing stranger, chose to live among them was a unique honor.

After a walk around the outskirts of the village, Jacoby and Boy would emerge from a trail above the piazza and join a narrow, shaded lane to the artisan's studio where Giovanni made the shoes for his family's shop while listening to his beloved Pearl Jam collection on compact discs. The two friends practiced their respective languages together, eager to learn the other's native tongue, but they did not speak of reuniting for another concert of Pearl Jam covers like the one they had performed at the last village festival. Such a gig was too spectacular, too rock & roll to try again. They had one legendary performance, and that was enough. Any other attempts would only diminish that singular event. Though, on occasion, they would play together in the studio or at the hotel.

On the way back to the piazza, Jacoby would stop in to see the village butcher, who greeted him with a bellowed "Ohhhh!" and affectionately called him "Johnny" in honor of the Americans who had helped liberate Florence from the Nazis when the butcher was just a boy. Adding to the charm of this reference was the fact that one "Johnny" had fallen in love with the daughter of the Floria-Zanobini family and escaped with her to America, and that they were Jacoby's grandparents on his mother's side. For Boy, the magic of the butcher shop was the scraps of meat that awaited him, along with a giant bone he could work the marrow out of and gnaw the surface of all afternoon while Jacoby was off to check on rehabilitation progress at the estate a few miles out of town.

On Bill's rusted motorino, Jacoby would take an access road a few miles then turn up a single lane road, that accommodated vehicles in both directions, under a canopy of birch and chestnut, the smell of old wood and turning leaves filling his nose as insects bounced off the face mask of his helmet and the air cooled with the rise in elevation. A wide, bumpy track of dirt led to a vast opening where a former abbey and cloisters had been converted into the village's consortium, a fattoria, or production center, for making wine and olive oil from the bounty of the surrounding hills and hollows, and there the Floria-Zanobini estate was located in all its former glory.

The fattoria was in good shape as it had operated consistently as the village's production site, and such a valuable entity was dutifully, even lovingly, maintained year round by a crew of men who lived in quarters on the ramparts of the estate that they would share with the migrants who arrived to help with the harvest. The exterior and immediate grounds around the fattoria were well kept, the equipment inside cleaned and updated regularly. It had been operated unofficially by the locals with permission of the estate, but now it was very officially in the hands of Paolo and his small cohort, along with Dolores as a supposed-to-be-silent, but-not-so-silent partner, who had plans to produce and market the products beyond local means, though her interests were overwhelmingly invested in her singular ownership of the villa itself.

It was an enormous edifice of 30 rooms spreading beyond the consortium on the area's highest ridge. The views outward were spectacular, of endless sky and rolling hills dotted with farmhouses, lined with vineyards and blanketed with forests. The view of the villa itself was not as inspiring: a jaundiced facade strewn with patches of moss, listing shutters, a roof of cracked Spanish tiles, a rusted fence of pointed iron, and grounds covered in overgrowth, felled trees and gorse. The back terrace was of cracked tiles leading to an emptied Olympic-sized pool, and the interior was almost as bad.

But there were signs of progress of late. Finally. No workers could be found in the summer as the country essentially shuts down in August and prepares for the shutdown in the months prior, especially with regard to physical labor when seasonal migrants don't even bother looking for work and wait for the harvest. Dolores had located a reliable contractor through her English friends with renovated properties such as her own, in the area of Tuscany so inhabited by the English it was sardonically referred to as "Chiantishire." The contractor and Jacoby had been in touch over the summer and met for coffee on a few occasions at the cafe.

He promised to begin in September, and, sure enough, scaffolding was erected toward the middle of the month and work began at, in what Jacoby would soon learn to be, an acceptable Italian pace. There were days when Jacoby arrived to find no workers at all, and some days with a skeleton crew and some days with a dozen men on site. His job was simply to report the progress to Dolores, and she seemed to be well aware of what constituted the Italian work ethic, at least in this part of the peninsula. Her expectations were in place with regard to completion as well, with no realistic end date in mind.

Jacoby, on the other hand, was damn eager for the completion since Dolores promised to hire him to manage the estate once it was converted into a luxury hotel. And Jacoby could live there, on the property once owned by his family, and it would be then that his redemption would be complete.

Chapter 5

There wasn't much work happening that day, a skeleton crew moving some scaffolding from a completed section of facade renovation to another that was being prepped for repair. The completed work was impressive, and Jacoby enjoyed watching the villa come back to life, albeit slowly.

Jacoby checked in on Bruna, the ancient property caretaker who had raised Filippo and had been so helpful in Bill and Jacoby's search for the matriarch. She lived alone within the vast, sparse interior of the villa and spent her days cooking for the workers, tending to the immediate grounds, and preparing the interior for its turn at rehabilitation.

Bruna spoke no English, and her Italian was of a dialect from her native Calabria, taxing Jacoby's ability to understand, so they mostly communicated through simple, concise sentences of greetings and farewells, and physical embrace, kisses on each cheek, warm hugs. As the Italian's said: baci e abbracci. Kisses and hugs.

Jacoby found Bruna out back, past the cracked terrace, beyond the border of cypress trees and umbrella pines, on her knees praying by the family mausoleum. It was a white marble unit that resembled a miniature version of grand palaces from Roman antiquity, complete with columns topped by ornate sculptures. Inside lay the family Floria-Zanobini, joined recently by the last living member of name, Jacoby's great grandmother. Bruna wiped away some tears and moved slowly to her feet to replace the wilted wild flowers at the base of the mausoleum with the fresh ones held in her withered hand. She made the sign of the cross and turned to find Jacoby behind her.

"Oh," she said, touching her chest. "Buongiorno, giovane."

Jacoby liked that she simply called him "young." He also liked bending down to kiss the soft cheeks of her tawny face that smelled of lilac. He liked to imagine her as the Italian grandmother he would have loved growing up. Bruna held Jacoby's hand and smiled with contrition. She motioned with her other hand toward the mausoleum in a recognition of finality.

"Triste," she said and bowed her head.

Jacoby agreed that it was sad, but he, for some reason, could not accept her sentiment of finality. The family did not feel finished to him, and he assumed that was his own ego and longing for the family that he convinced himself he was a part of, and technically was, but there was and would never be any official recognition. He thought of his own mother, laid to rest, he believed, in New Jersey, and wondered if he could somehow, at some point, have her body exhumed and moved here. This was the lack of finality tugging at Jacoby, he assumed, as he walked Bruna back to the villa and then steered the motorino out of the countryside and toward the city of Florence to meet his beloved Helen Dempsey for a dinner date.

·   ·   ·

The trip by scooter was roughly 20 minutes out of his rural community and into the uninspired ramparts of Florence proper, of commercial areas and low-slung apartment buildings where residents, not fortunate enough to live in the city-center itself, made their homes. It reminded Jacoby of pre-gentrified areas in the outer boroughs of New York or the small cities outside of Boston. He was happy not to be distracted by the surroundings as traffic picked up and he was vulnerable on the motorino, mostly avoiding the other two-wheeled operators who zipped around without code or concern. The roundabouts were particularly chaotic, and he counted three he needed to navigate before the river came into view with the city beyond. Instead of entering through one of the portals where walls once stood, Jacoby would take a winding road under a canopy of umbrella pines, past regal and shaded estates, up to Piazzale Michelangelo from where he first set eyes on the city of Florence.

The inconvenient parking spot was justified by Jacoby's nostalgia for the stunning view of the city, one that offered a reminder of the wonder he felt upon first glance and still felt these many times after, but parking above the city was also his excuse to avoid the vehicular pandemonium within the heart of the city itself.

The sun, a giant egg yolk, was considering its descent beyond the hills west of the city, casting a hazy pallor over the towers and domes and facades, turning the surface of the Arno into a sheen of gold. Birds were chattering in the hedges and trees. Jacoby could smell the honey made by monks in a nearby monastery. Tourist season was nearly over, so the piazzale was not crowded. A slight breeze lifted Jacoby's bangs as he took his first steps down the switchback trail that led to his favorite place on earth, a place he had only known for months but felt like he had lived his entire life. If asked, he wanted to say he was from Florence. He so wanted to be asked and to tell everybody.

The walk down, for a fit and agile Jacoby, was no more than ten minutes, though he often passed others who had stopped to rest or regain balance. He always smiled when remembering the time a tipsy and overdressed Dolores had to navigate the ramp's more precarious passages. He also appreciated her introducing him to this means of entering the city.

At the bottom was the tower of San Niccolò in the eponymous and sleepy neighborhood. Jacoby liked the narrow, cobbled streets and the tiny doors of quaint homes within faded pastel facades, and the little cars, Fiat Cinquecenti, that looked more like toys than automobiles but remained perfect for navigating the ancient, serpentine streets with very limited parking. Cats wandered without worry and slept within doorways. The shops were still open and elegant Florentines browsed on their way home from work, carefully choosing the freshest ingredients for that night's dinner.

Jacoby tried to walk slowly, like a true Florentine, with his hands clasped behind him and his head held high, but he was anxious to see

Helen and aware that his inconvenient parking preference and its subsequent walk cost him precious time. So he passed many residents at a brisk clip on his course for the quartiere of Santo Spirito in Oltrarno, the "other" side of the Arno. Across from the Pitti Palace, he turned down a minuscule lane, lined with artisan lace and leather shops, that would eventually, after numerous twists and turns, open to the charming Piazza della Passera where Helen lived above a tiny shop. She would be waiting for him in the piazza, on a bench where they had martinis on their very first date and near where they would later that same magical night share a first kiss under a sky exploding with fireworks.

"Hello, my Jacoby Pines," she said like always upon his arrival, uncrossing her legs to stand and give him a sharp peck on the lips, followed by a long hug. She wore a sleeveless white blouse tied at her navel, gray Capri pants and classic oxford shoes the color of cognac. Helen worked six days a week throughout the spring and to the very end of the tourist season in autumn, maximizing her income while it was available. Her demanding schedule only allowed for bi-weekly visits from Jacoby. She had yet to come out to the village.

"Hi," Jacoby said, nuzzling her blond bob, savoring his limited exposure to his fledgling love.

"Were you hurrying?" Helen asked as they parted.

Jacoby tented his wrinkled dress shirt, moist with perspiration. "Yeah, sorry," he said.

"No worries," Helen said, squinting slightly in preparation of saying something risque. "I'll just have to give you a bath later."

They'd spent more than a few occasions immersed in bubbles in Helen's claw-foot tub. Jacoby smiled and flapped his shirt again. "That's why I ran all the way here."

"You're clever," Helen said. "And I'm hungry. Shall we eat?"

"My favorite question," Jacoby said. "After an aperitivo?"

Helen smacked him playfully on the chest. "You're becoming so Italian."

"I'm working on it," Jacoby said.

"Well, don't work on it too hard, otherwise you'll end up leaving me for your mother."

Jacoby looked down and away. Helen took his hand. "I'm sorry. Did that upset you? The mention of your mother."

"No, no. It's fine," Jacoby said, taking Helen's other hand. They faced each other like children, clasped by all four hands, covered in the slanted sun of a fading autumn afternoon. "It's just that I've been thinking about my mother a lot as of late, more than I ever have. It's weird."

"Well," Helen said with kindness and a touch of pomp. "You are among her ancestors, after all, if not literally any more, certainly in a spiritual sense. My god, that old villa alone must be full of ghosts. There's probably a family reunion floating around at all hours."

A church bell rang six times. Doves cooed in the eaves and pigeons plucked around the piazza's stone surface. A few people passed. Jacoby nodded and looked Helen in the eye. "Yeah," he said. "Makes sense."

"Did I tell you I was brilliant?" Helen asked with a tilted chin.

"Once or twice."

"You know what else is brilliant?"

"Tell me?"

"A spritz! Especially on an evening like this."

"Sounds good."

Helen clicked her heels. "Campari or Aperol?"

"Aperol."

"I'll get Campari and we can exchange straws."

Helen dashed off to the nearby bar with it's doors opened to the street. Jacoby sat on what he considered "their" bench and watched a kid kick a soccer ball against a wall of pastel aglow in autumn sun. Helen returned with two balloon glasses full of ice and stuck with straws, the liquid ruby colored in one and orange-amber in the other. They chinked glasses and sat back on the bench, Helen tucked under Jacoby's extended arm along the slats of the bench.

They sipped their drinks in silence, exchanging glasses at one point. Even though Jacoby did not love the medicinal flavor of Aperol, he did appreciate the refreshing combination of bitter and bubbly, which also, as intended, fired up his appetite.

"Where are we eating?" he asked when the drinks were nearly finished.

Helen sat up. "There's a place by the river I've been wanting to try, right on Via Santo Spirito. It's actually sort of new and trendy."

"New? Trendy?" Jacoby asked. "Where are we, New York?"

"Oh, stop," she said. "You can't eat cucina tipica every night."

"Says who?"

"Says me," Helen said. "I need to be on top of these things, you know, to recommend to my clients."

With a quick slurp, Jacoby finished the diluted remnants of his spritz. "So this is like research."

"Yes," Helen said with a hint of formality. "Let's call it that."

"Works for me," Jacoby said and stood. He held out a hand to Helen, and did not let go as they returned the glasses and walked the hushed streets toward the river as swallows took to the last light gathered high above the rooftops.

Chapter 6

The restaurant was spanking new by Florence's standards, opened only a few years earlier as opposed to the majority of city restaurants which had been in business for generations with a menu that dated back to previous centuries. The interior had slightly vaulted ceilings with lots of dark wood trim, exposed brick, and antique bric-a-brac on the walls, including a framed photograph of Ernest Hemingway (of which Jacoby thoroughly approved), and shelves lined with bottles of wine and local products. The tables and chairs were refurbished, and the room, accessorized by young and stylish patrons, wreaked of the faux-hipster vibe that Jacoby hated in Brooklyn but could tolerate in Italy, especially since the food was fantastic and the mood so pleasant. And the wine list, a rarity, included bottles from all over the peninsula.

Jacoby loved that Helen liked to share plates as opposed to ordering separately and tasting each other's choices. The latter, inevitably, being too much food and much less fun. They shared, over glasses of prosecco, a mixed plate of cured meats, young cheeses and grilled vegetables under oil. A plate of handmade pasta with spicy nduja and aged pecorino was washed down with a carafe of fruity yet forward Barbaresco from Piemonte. Wild duck with roasted grapes paired perfectly with a carafe of Rosso Piceno from Le Marche. For dessert, Jacoby watched Helen rapturously eat a ramekin of mascarpone cheese and strawberries while he sipped a local grappa.

After splitting the check, they went to Ponte alla Carraia and sat on the parapet above the middle arch to watch the sun smolder over the bridges and buildings to the west and eventually settle behind the mountains beyond. In the sifting darkness, they walked back to Helen's apartment and had that bath she had promised before sleeping soundly with the windows open to the tiny piazza below. In the morning, Jacoby woke early, got dressed, kissed a dozing Helen on the forehead and hurried back through the nearly empty streets of Oltrarno in the fledgling light to trek up the incline to Piazzale Michelangelo and hop on Bill's motorino to rush against traffic back to the village, retrieve Boy from Nicoletta, who kept him on nights that Jacoby stayed in town, walk up the hill with his dog to the barn to clean up, get dressed and return to the village for work. No problem.

The only complication on this particular morning was that Jacoby had to pack for his trip to Rome with Bill, a task made all the more difficult by the lack of clarity on how long they would be gone or even what he personally would be doing while there besides accompanying Bill. Still, Jacoby had much faith in his new friend, and he was anxious to see the capital city of this magnificent country that he now considered home. Jacoby's only suitcase was the crappy Samsonite that he brought to Italy with the intention of staying a year, so he packed it up with his best clothes and hoped he wouldn't be gone for that long.

Jacoby had told Helen, over dinner, of his plans with Bill, and she agreed that it was smart to do business in Italy in person. He had asked her to join them, but she was booked with tours at the museum during the last few weeks of the dwindling tourist season. She had, though, promised Jacoby a trip together in a few weeks, which she would start planning while he was away. He promised himself, that no matter what happened in Rome, he would be back for Helen and her plans at the latest.

He was also going to miss Boy. The dog, even after a single night's absence, reacted upon his return as if Jacoby had been gone for years. Nicoletta said that he waited by her door and whimpered each night before falling asleep, and this broke Jacoby's heart as much as it uplifted it, knowing he was so loved by such a sweet creature. He was going to arrange a lot of scraps and bones from the butcher so Nicoletta could spoil Boy each day that Jacoby was away and stay connected through their shared ritual and mutual love of food.

Bill, in a crisp dress shirt, pleated slacks and leather loafers, looked refreshed and enthusiastic. The travel bag, hooked over his shoulder, filled Jacoby with relief about the extent of their journey. A cab picked them up in the village and wound up the hill to the barn to get Jacoby's suitcase before taking the access road down from the hills and into Florence. Jacoby's heart arched high up in his chest and his breath was short as they left the village with Nicoletta and Giovanni waving, the latter holding the leash tight on a lunging and yelping Boy. So distracted by minor sorrow, Jacoby did not notice the loaded hunter's jeep pass them in a whoosh toward the village.

·　　·　　·

The town car crossed the River Arno and navigated the city streets with requisite care and abandon, jockeying among the motorino and motorcycles and small cars on the busy road that spanned the circumference of the city on the grounds where walls once stood for protection. The immediate outskirts of the city were uninspiring, and Jacoby brooded a bit, missing his dog and his girlfriend and his new home, wishing he was not accompanying Bill on a boring task, but his dread and self-pity was belied by a sense he could not ignore that, in general, going places was a good thing and, in particular, this trip felt promising. And he knew, if nothing else, he would be back and would be so happy to return.

Santa Maria Novella train station was vast and full of light, the mezzanine level feeling modern and, therefore, somewhat foreign within such an ancient city. The midday, weekday, off-season timing left the station uncrowded and nearly silent. Jacoby was relieved not to deal with the sensory chaos of crowds in unfamiliar territory. He waited with their bags near a news kiosk in the middle of the station while Bill purchased the tickets. Two young men in military uniforms stood guard nearby holding massive weapons across their narrow chests. A middle-aged couple were conversing while studying the train schedule, and Jacoby engaged in his habit of eavesdropping in attempts to decipher the language.

Jacoby was having a hard time with the Italian language. He obviously needed to learn the language of his new homeland, for practical purposes and especially if he was going to work in the hospitality industry, but he also enjoyed the anonymity of someone not privy to the words of others. It was liberating to be free from the requirement of conversation or just from overhearing all the stupid things people say to each other. Not knowing the specific words used in Italian but being surrounded by the sound of the language was like the accompaniment of beautiful music without knowing the specifics of notes and orchestration. There was a point when he vowed to just learn the language of food and wine, to know how to read a menu and wine list. Nothing more. But that was a foolish notion, he knew, though it was where he began, paying close attention to all things gastronomic while eavesdropping on occasion as well. Both practices were possible in restaurants, and this thought, while standing in the din of Florence's train station, reminded Jacoby that he was hungry.

Bill returned with tickets and said they had an hour to kill before their train arrived. Jacoby suggested lunch. Bill smiled. They checked their bags in a luggage office and hit the uncrowded streets of the sleepy quarter that shared a name with its train station and most notable church. Its ornate facade of alternating green and white marble was shared by many of Florence's most famous churches, including the Duomo whose massive, crushed-orange cupola could be seen above the low-slung roof line in the direction which Jacoby and Bill walked.

"Are we going to the Duomo?" Jacoby asked.

"No, dear boy," Bill said, his head active as he walked, taking in all of his surroundings. "We are going to a different kind of church."

"What type of church is that?" Jacoby asked, keeping up with his brisk-walking friend on narrow streets, stepping off the sidewalk at times to avoid passersby.

"A church of meat," Bill said.

Jacoby put his hands together in front of his chest and said, "Hallelujah."

Chapter 7

Trattoria Mario, across an open square from the Mercato Centrale, was the opposite of the place he had eaten with Helen the night before. Entered through a small storefront covered in press clippings, it was old-school Italy, under a low-ceiling, cramped and of basic decor. Communal tables crowded the floor space. Italian memorabilia and lots of support for the city's soccer team covered the walls. The harried waitresses, paper hats and matching uniforms, ferried trays stacked with food and clutched carafes of house wine. Men in white Ts and stained aprons were behind a glass partition, busy working flaming grills, filling plates and bowls, moving non-stop, talking loudly to each other and the waitresses. The room reeked of meat smoke and wine-soaked floors.

"Oh, yeah," Jacoby said as they stood in the busy foyer and waited for their table. His sluicing saliva glands filling his mouth.

"I thought you'd approve," Bill said, looking around the bustling hall with content.

"A little crowded, though. No?" Jacoby asked, aware of Bill's disdain for the burdens of rampant tourism, especially the overcrowding.

Bill faced Jacoby and clutched the inside of his arm. "Are you kidding? This is nothing! During the season, there's a line out the door and around the block. We practically have the place to ourselves, in terms of Trattoria Mario."

"OK," Jacoby conceded. "Must be good."

"You shall see."

They were soon seated at a long table in the middle of the room alongside a group of four newly-arrived American exchange students, all girls, who chatted them up and drank house wine at lunch and gushed about the lifestyle of "Firenze." Jacoby wanted to be cynical, to roll his eyes at the silly Americans all a blush over Florence, but he knew exactly how they felt. Bill did most of the talking, sharing with them all sorts of insider information, which they tapped into their phones and thanked him for profusely. Jacoby shared Helen's information for tours of the Uffizi and wished he had asked her to join them for lunch. Jacoby also wished for the opportunity to practice his Italian by ordering, but the room was too loud and the waitresses too busy, so he left it up to Bill.

The girls had only sat moments before the two men, so Bill took the liberty of first explaining to the young Americans that each meal out in Italy did not require four individual courses, and then he ordered for the whole table, after inquiring about their preferences and dietary restrictions.

"Allora," Bill began by saying to a smiling waitress, no doubt aware that he would not be ordering in the tortured Italian of a tourist. "Ribollita per due. Ragu per quattro. Poi, tacchino arrosto per due e bistecca per il resto con fagioli all'uccelletto per tutti. E vino rosso per il tavalo."

"Della casa?"

"Certamente."

Jacoby was pleased to have, rather easily, translated the menu of Ribollita, a bread and bean and cabbage soup, and roasted turkey for the two who did not eat red meat; and ragu of meat followed by the famous Florentine steak for those who did not abstain from the carnivorous splendor of the thick, Tuscan porterhouse cut from specially raised cows. The table would share white beans and the house red wine.

The two courses were served rather quickly and the wine went and was replenished even faster. The girls were quaffing it up, but Jacoby and Bill sipped more responsibly as they had travel plans. The girls were off from school, as it was Friday, with no plans for the day beyond a boozy, decadent lunch. They directed their attention mostly to Bill and his avuncular charms, and this suited Jacoby fine as he was able to focus on the food, which was very good, especially the bistecca and white beans, one of his favorite Tuscan meals among many favorite Tuscan meals. The wine was fine, but far better than its price, which was less than bottled water in New York restaurants.

Bill insisted on paying the whole tab and then recommended the Hotel Floria-Zanobini for when the girls' parents came to visit, giving Jacoby the idea of soliciting all of the universities in town who hosted students from abroad. It could be an appealing option to staying in the city, one that could also include guided tours of Florence and the Tuscan countryside as well as cooking classes of 'cucina tipica' in the hotel's kitchen with Bill.

They left the trattoria together and Bill and Jacoby wandered back to the train station after Bill directed the girls to a nearby gelato shop that should not be missed.

.   .   .

The station was busier than before with trains arriving and departing in the hours after lunch. Still, it was not difficult to retrieve their luggage and board their train on time. They had seats in Business Class, per Bill's insistence, and Jacoby immediately understood the benefits of a small upcharge, as their compartment was nearly empty, unlike the others crowded with indigenous travelers and tourists from all over the world. The seats in Business Class were leather and spacious with lots of leg room.

Bill, as he often did, with his palms splayed on his thighs, looked off into nowhere, still and silent as their dormant train. He was asleep before the locomotive hissed and lurched the cars into motion. Jacoby wondered what Bill thought of in his pensive moments or what he dreamed of during his frequent naps. Of course, he knew: Love that is lost never goes away.

The train passed through some industrial sections of the city before the countryside opened up in its postcard splendor of olive groves and vineyards. Trees whizzed by the windows under the sapphire sky that stretched to infinity. Even through a window, traveling at rapid speed, the light of Italy was surreal, as if illuminating the world in a way reflective of all the beauty it held. The light seemed to be singing, made radiant by the magnificence of this glorious peninsula. Il Bel Paese. The beautiful country.

Jacoby grew sleepy from the wine-soaked lunch. And he drifted off thinking of the wonderful embrace of a small break at midday that the Italians, in most parts of the country, still practiced. Riposo. A short rest, after a long, slow lunch. And this was not a special occasion or a holiday or even a weekend. It was every day. How appropriate and civilized. How un-American. Hurry back to your desk after a quick lunch. Get right to it. Work. Work. Work. Jacoby was not dismissive of his home country. He understood how America operated and why. It was the culture. The ethos. A lot of good, to not just the country but the world, came from the American way. It worked for many but not for him. And what a contrast to the quality of life he enjoyed in Italy. He was right to embrace this land and its practices. This is where he belonged, and he counted his blessings as the rushing train rocked him to sleep.

Chapter 8

Bill woke Jacoby as the train entered the outskirts of Rome. The squat, concrete buildings beyond the windows were drab, lacking imagination with faded and scarred facades marked by crude graffiti. The vibe reminded Jacoby of the many small American cities that had lost their industry and faded into blight. The association with defeat saddened him as he had yet to see a part of Italy, up to this point, that did not inspire wonder, if not awe.

"Don't worry, young man," Bill said, reading the slight sign of duress on Jacoby's face. "These were all built by the Fascists in the previous century with the intention of stifling imagination. You will surely find the work of their predecessors far more inspiring."

Jacoby liked that he and Bill were so in sync, that they got each other in such a profound way. Through his itinerant and often lonely childhood and adolescence, Jacoby didn't have many close friends and certainly never one of the "best" variety. He was also an only child, and that of a melancholy widower, with no cousins or extended family of any kind that he knew of. His connections to other people were limited by that reality, so he was particularly appreciative of his unconventional bond to a man more than twice his age but of such similar nature. They often had to explain that they were not relatives or May-December lovers. They were friends. And Jacoby knew that true friendship with Bill was another gift that Italy offered him.

"After you," Bill said with a gesture toward the aisle.

The train had gone underground and arrived at the station. Jacoby nodded to Bill and took his suitcase from the overhead rack. It was too big for contemporary travel though it did, at least, have wheels. Jacoby rolled the suitcase down the aisle toward the open door and carried it down the steps. The platform was cool and bustling, and the sound in the distance of the main terminal implied a crowded, cavernous theater. Jacoby followed a step behind Bill who looked around eagerly, as if able to recognize everyone and everything.

The main terminal of Termini Station was indeed vast, but there was, like Santa Maria Novella, much slanted light and space. Still, it was clear to Jacoby just by comparing train stations that Rome was a big "C" city compared to the quaint urban environs of Florence. More in every sensory way. He was thinking of a New York to Boston comparison as they navigated the pedestrians crossing their path at various angles on their way in and out of the station's main entrance.

A slightly acrid smell met Jacoby outside. It was actually less noticeable than the air quality in Florence, which was by no means smoggy but had difficulty ventilating pollution, being sunken and surrounded by hills. The air was warmer than Florence, too. The sun slapping at his forearms and the back of his neck. Indian Summer weather, a reprise of heat in transitioning seasons. The clouds were bulbous and bright white and holding a shade of ozone in their bellies. Cars and buses swung around the entrance drive, and the open expanse revealed a busy traffic circle beyond the umbrella pines. With his travel bag over a shoulder, Bill led Jacoby by the arm to a taxi stand where they waited silently in a modest line for their car.

Bill seemed serene. Hands in front pockets, chin up, looking around. He was not pointing out every detail or reminiscing. Not attempting to establish his local bonafides. Jacoby remembered that Bill used to give guided tours of Rome, and that he once complained about how eager most American tourists were to just consume the city in every way, so Jacoby resisted his desire to ask a few basic questions. He would engage Rome at Bill's pace, which seemed promising.

The sleek Mercedes sedan taxi maneuvered around the traffic circle and down a wide avenue lined on both sides with large buildings of modest design. It seemed grand but generic to Jacoby, like

Broadway in Manhattan or the European cities he'd seen in movies, and Jacoby was struck by a ping of panic: Was it possible that Rome was lame? Overrated? Overrun by packs of stealth little thieves as rumored. Maybe Florence was the only special city in this country and Tuscany the only special region. Was he going to have to pretend to be impressed so as not to hurt Bill's feelings? Pores opened around his neck and the discomfort of being displaced crept into his belly.

And then they veered around a bend and the first site of antiquity appeared in ancient columns and what appeared to be ruins in the near distance. And was that the top of the Colosseum? Jacoby sat up. After another wide turn, they descended past the high gates of palaces and elegant hotels with massive flags out front, and then down into the flats where the sidewalks grew crowded. Sophisticated residents and typical tourists crossed the street in front of the taxi that had stopped at a light. Once in motion, the most magnificent building Jacoby had ever seen, brilliant white and majestic, with massive columns and landings and statues, was suddenly across a piazza of grass bedded with flowers. The expanse seemed to shimmer and the monument of a building appeared to erupt out of the earth.

Abandoning his plan at decorum, Jacoby blurted, "Holy shit! What is that?"

"That, my boy, is the Altare della Patria, the Alter of the Fatherland. It is colloquially referred to as the wedding cake or the typewriter because of the color and the shape."

Jacoby heard Bill's answer but asked for a repetition.

"It is officially dedicated to Vittorio Emanuele II, in honor of the unification of Italy in 1861 under his rule as king," Bill said. "We Romans refer to it as the Vittoriano."

Jacoby felt stupid and was afraid to ask but did anyway. "Italy's only been a country since 1861?"

Bill put his hand on Jacoby's forearm. "That surprises a lot of people," he said. "What we know as Italy has existed far longer than that, obviously, but the various regions were not unified, existing as separate city states, until the unification."

"I was going to say," Jacoby joked, trying to use deprecation to cover his shame at being poorly educated in world history.

"It's OK," Bill assured him. "Most Americans arrive here with limited understanding of Italy beyond its food, and even that is focused on cuisine of the southern regions from where the immigrants derived."

Not wanting to further explore his own ignorance, Jacoby leaned toward the window to gawk at the incredible building. Bill asked the driver to abandon their existing route. The car turned left down a small street and came back on a wide avenue to the side of the Wedding Cake, from where it joined traffic and followed a curving and busy road that passed ruins and afforded a quick view of the tree-lined banks of Tiber River before joining a stretch, bordered by crumbling ruins and a variety of pines on each side, that ran parallel to the Circus Maximus where chariot races were once held and Bill, in a previous decade, had seen the Rolling Stones in concert. The car took a hard left and ran between a park and a hill marked by more ruins.

"Wow," Jacoby joked. "This town is old."

"That is the Palatine Hill," Bill pointed to the left. "Where Rome was born."

"Rome was born?"

"You know the story of Remus and Romulus. Don't you?"

"Remus and Romulus?" Jacoby said the names he'd never heard. "Sounds like a law firm."

Bill laughed as the car circled around the Colosseum and Jacoby leaned down to see as much of its crumbled grandeur as he could, even turning to look out the back window as the car cruised down another stretch that featured much of the Roman Forum to the right and ruin-stacked hills to the left before coming up on the other side of the Wedding Cake and Piazza Venezia. The white building looked even the more surreal beneath a pristine blue sky of a mid-to-late afternoon in the heart of autumn.

"We have much to show you," Bill said, crossing his arms and nodding as the car turned down a main thoroughfare pinched between stoic palaces of pastel facades that took up entire blocks. "And we've just begun."

Jacoby was thrilled and so glad he came along on this excursion to Rome that would soon, in Italian time, become an adventure.

Chapter 9

As the sedan cruised the regal avenue, Jacoby had his first prosaic observation of Rome: It offered a lot of sky overhead. Almost all of the buildings were uniform in their height of four or so floors, even with the tops of the exotic trees, a vertical consistency maintained throughout the city, only interrupted, ever so slightly, by the domes of modest churches that barely breached the consistent roof lines. Thanks to the ruins and some obvious urban planning, there were also open spaces and wide avenues, though he'd soon discover the tiny, shaded lanes - some no wider than extended arms - that slithered throughout the city center.

The buildings themselves, squat and formidable, of carved stone and pastel plaster, captured the essence of the city in its dichotomy. It was definitely a big city, more in every way as compared to Florence, but still so informed by the order and beauty and history of Italy. Jacoby was now up on the seat as far as he could go, peering through the front window at the urban majesty on display, fascinated by each majestic corner. Past a baroque church, the car turned off the boulevard and wobbled over cobblestones on tiny streets lined with hotels, shops and eateries. It stopped at the mouth of a large piazza filled with people and light, in front of a restaurant on the corner with a woman at a large table by an open partition making pasta by hand.

Bill paid the taxi fare and chatted with the pasta maker as Jacoby secured his suitcase from the trunk and bumped it over the cobblestones to join Bill as the taxi warbled away down a shaded side street.

"Buongiorno," the pasta maker greeted Jacoby. She was beautifully round in the face with kind eyes and dimples when she smiled.

"Buongiorno," Jacoby said and asked, encouraged by her sweet countenance, what she was doing. "Che cosa fai?"

He told himself in that moment that he would be brave in Rome and speak as much Italian as possible, and he breathed a quick breath when the woman opened her mouth to respond to his inquiry.

"Strozzapreti, fatto a mano," she said.

Jacoby sighed. He had no clue what she said beyond "fatto" which was the past tense of "made" but he wondered why she would be speaking in the past tense about what she was doing now. He looked at Bill.

"She's making strozzapreti by hand," he explained. "Fatto a mano is an expression meaning handmade. Strozzapreti is the type of pasta she's making. It's a sort of elongated cavatelli and common throughout central Italy."

"Oh," is all Jacoby could say as he watched the woman take thick ribbons of pale-yellow pasta and roll them with her hands loosely, width-wise, into imperfect tubes. Not only did he have to learn the language but all of the other stuff, too, like expressions and pasta variations. He was up for it, even though the learning process would be awkward if not embarrassing. He was already embarrassed, after four months in Italy, by how little he spoke and less he understood. The Italians spoke so fast, and most - upon recognizing his non-native tongue - wanted to speak English with him. He felt especially defeated in those moments when he sucked up his courage and addressed a stranger in fledgling Italian only for them to respond in practiced English. Sometimes they even beat him to it by speaking to him in English before he opened his mouth like he had "American who sucks at Italian" stamped on his forehead. The worst was when people expressed frustration with his efforts, which was rare but especially devastating. That sucked, but he always vowed to persevere.

Jacoby was able to practice in the village where few spoke English, most frequently with Giovanni, but surely in Rome, as in Florence,

English was a second language, especially for those he encountered in the hospitality industry who didn't have time for the tourist eager to impress and practice.

Bill put a hand on Jacoby's shoulder, as if sensing his consternation. "We will make a point of getting you up to speed in Italian on all things pasta in particular and things Italian in general while we are here. I promise."

Jacoby was aware that Bill preferred to speak English with him for various reasons, so he didn't push his friend to be a teacher, though he was glad for the offer and vowed to make it as painless as possible. And even fun.

"Strozzapreti," Jacoby said.

"Well said," Bill responded. "Fun to say, and even better to eat."

"Yes, please," Jacoby responded, nodding his head with exaggeration and looking at the women busy rolling pasta.

"Let's get settled first," Bill said and walked toward a side street going away from the restaurant in the direction the taxi had gone. Only a few doors down, Bill stopped and pulled a key ring from his bag and broke out one of his favorite expressions. "And here we are."

Chapter 10

The door was of faded wood and small, certainly by Italian standards. There was an archway next to the door which opened to a small courtyard, cool and shaded, with a simple fountain in the middle and colorful front doors accessed on the ground level and up wrought iron staircases. The walls of the apartments were covered in ivy and the window sills had planters with dangling green leaves. Motorcycles and bicycles were idle along the walls.

The faded door off the street opened to a tiny foyer with an exposed bulb. The walls were of stone and met a stairwell of concrete. The dank smell of minerals filled Jacoby's nose. The metal door of the electrical box was open and Bill began flicking fuse switches.

"What are you doing?" Jacoby asked.

"Turning on our lights."

"I thought we were staying in a hotel?"

"This is a hotel," Bill said, facing Jacoby and smiling wide. "At least in the secretive world of the Floria-Zanobinis. It is far less recognized than the property we acquired in Florence, and I'm not surprised it hasn't been discovered as an asset by the authorities."

"Why are they so secretive?" Jacoby asked.

"That's a very good question," Bill asked. "And one I've never had answered, though it dates back to their former status as powerful merchants and a need, for some reason, to be clandestine. It certainly has served us well. Don't you think?"

"I'll say," Jacoby quipped while pondering the mysteries of his ancestors.

Bill walked briskly up the dimly lit stairwell and Jacoby had to carry his suitcase in front of his chest to navigate the narrow passageway. He began to breathe a little heavy on the third floor and was nearly out of breath and sweating around his neck by the meager fifth floor landing. He put down his luggage and waited on a step with a hand against the cold wall, catching his breath, feeling his sweat dry and wondering what was happening, though he had ultimate faith in Bill, who was trying various keys on numerous locks.

"Allora," he said as the last tumbler rolled and the door opened. Jacoby foisted up his suitcase and followed Bill into an unlit room full of fading daylight. It was a modest space with immediate entry into a nicely furnished living area. Jacoby left his suitcase and followed Bill through the room and past an alcove kitchen with a miniature refrigerator and stove, toward closed curtains that when parted revealed a terrace as large as the apartment's interior.

"And this is why we choose to stay here," Bill said. He unlocked the door of glass and slid it open. Late afternoon air, holding some remnants of warmth but informed by the approaching night, rushed in and filled Jacoby's taxed lungs with delicious relief. He followed Bill out onto the terracotta surface and admired the roof line of Rome, of uniformed Spanish tiles and terraces everywhere, each adorned with lush greenery and outdoor furniture, partitions for privacy and umbrellas for shade. The sun was on its way down, and the horizon took on an orange gloaming beneath the fading blue.

"This works," Jacoby said, his eyes blooming as he walked the surface and marveled at the view.

Their terrace, among the largest in sight, of two levels, had wrought iron furniture of chairs and a small table and a larger one for group dining on the upper level. There was a grilling apparatus carved into stone and some potted cactus plants around the perimeter. A din from the direction they were dropped off by the taxi was audible and Jacoby leaned against the railing in hopes of a view.

"What is that anyway?" he asked Bill, pointing in the direction of the sound.

"Campo de' Fiori," he said. "My favorite piazza in all of Rome."

"Can we go?"

"Of course," Bill said. "Let's get settled and cleaned up, then take a quick tour of our immediate vicinity."

"And eat some strozzapreti," Jacoby added.

"And eat some strozzapreti," Bill agreed.

. . .

Dusk had begun to settle as they left their apartment building. Campo de' Fiori was mere steps away from their door. The pasta maker was not in the window, but the restaurant, Osteria da Fortunata, was fairly busy for an off-season weeknight. Bill stepped inside and reserved a table to be safe. The piazza hummed in the sifting twilight with groups of local teens on and around the modest fountains, street vendors demonstrating the goods they hocked to tourists beleaguered after a full day of touring, and elegant Roman professionals taking an aperitivo at the cafes that lined the piazza's perimeter.

The two American expats strolled past a salumeria where Jacoby approached the fearsome head of wild boar hung above the door.

"Hey," Jacoby said. "Looks like our guy."

"Indeed," Bill agreed. "Though surely not slain as heroically."

"True. True," Jacoby said decorously. "Nor prepared into such a fine ragu."

Bill nodded in return. "How about an aperitivo of our own before dinner?"

Jacoby threw out his hands, smirked and asked why not. "Perchè no?"

They sat at a small table at a cafe on the piazza's far corner, near a trattoria Bill recommended for Jacoby's lunch the next day.

"Where will you be?"

"Bouncing around, I imagine, from government agency to government agency."

Their drinks arrived and the conversation stopped as the smiling waitress placed two Aperol spritzes on the small table. Stars began to appear above the roof line. The men raised their glasses and toasted. "Cin. Cin," Jacoby said.

"Cin. Cin," Bill echoed.

Jacoby preferred the bitter of the Aperol as opposed to the sweet of Campari, though the ruby color of the latter was of more appeal as the color of his spritz reminded him of a sports drink.

They sipped their aperitivo and watched Rome on parade. It was noisy and busy but not tense. Almost harmonious.

"Hey," Jacoby remembered a previous thought interrupted by the arrival of their drinks. "Won't I be busy bouncing around from government agency to government agency right alongside you?"

"Why no," Bill said. "I wouldn't hear of it."

Jacoby grew puzzled but knew enough to have faith in his friend. "Then why am I here? What will I do all day?"

Bill straightened up and inched his chair toward Jacoby. "You are here for two very important reasons. One is to keep me company in the mornings and evenings as this city holds many memories for me, and being here alone could be too painful, personally yes, but also with regard to carrying out the important task at hand. Two is for you, dear boy, to explore this magnificent city and learn to love it like I do as you will surely spend much time here in the coming years."

"Why do you say that?"

"Because you're young and urbane."

"No way, man," Jacoby said with feigned pomp and a tap on the tabletop. "I'm a Florentine! Forza Firenze! Forza Firenze!"

Bill leaned back and crossed his hands in front of his chest. "Your loyalty to Florence is admirable, but Rome has so much to offer. You'll see."

Jacoby got Bill's point and was reminded of Helen's talk of frequent travel in the off season. He thought of coming here with her, and he just thought of her.

"So I'm just going to walk around all day?" he asked Bill.

"Well, I wouldn't say it like that. We will take a cornetto and caffè together each day, in this very bar, where I will lay out an itinerary for you. Over dinner, after an aperitivo, you will tell me all about your glorious day."

"That sounds good."

"I imagine it does," Bill said. "But there's only one condition."

"And what's that?"

"That you eavesdrop."

"What? On who?"

"The Italians," Bill said. "I learned the language, in part, by watching Italian soap operas on television. Here, you will see, the soap opera is on display in real time."

That made sense to Jacoby. The Italians did all seem like performers in a soap opera with their high style and flare for the dramatic in the way they talked and the way they walked. "OK," he said. "I'll eavesdrop on the Italians and hope to hear something juicy."

"Oh, you will, especially here in Rome," Bill said. "It's just a matter of whether you understand it or not."

Jacoby flattened his lips in contrition at the challenge as the waitress returned to see if they wanted another drink. "And you must speak as often as possible," Bill added, motioning to the waitress. "Starting right now."

Jacoby took a breath and looked into the waitresses brown eyes. "No, grazie," he said. "Ho fame. Il conto, per favore."

The waitress smiled and made for the register.

"Very nice," Bill said. "Telling people you are hungry and asking for a check, politely, I might add, will get you very far."

"Grazie," Jacoby responded and rubbed his belly.

"Now let's take care of that hunger," Bill added with a sly wink.

Chapter 11

After a tour of the piazza's outer reaches, in the cool of an autumn evening, they were back at the corner from which they entered and soon seated at Osteria da Fortunata. The room, smelling of pasta sauces and roasted meat and espresso, was well lit and half full, designed for tourists with the rows of tightly arranged tables covered in butcher's paper and the name of the establishment on the ceramic plates and water glasses and decanters. The waiters kept a collective, macho banter that Jacoby found annoying.

"This place is a little touristy, no?" he asked Bill discretely once they were seated, per Bill's request, in a far corner, away from the main cluster of diners.

"Oh, it's a lot touristy," Bill said. "But the pasta is good, and I felt like staying close to home on our first night."

"Makes sense," he said. "Totally fine with me."

They sat side by side so both men could see the room. A bearded and bravo waiter with dark hair and a dark beard and dark hair flowing from his unbuttoned dress shirt plopped a basket of bread on the table and walked away all while having a conversation with a coworker on the other side of the room. Bill said, in a slightly raised voice, something to his back and then turned to face Jacoby with a bemused smile on his face.

"Now, let's get you started in the basics of cucina Romana," he said.

Jacoby rubbed his hands together. "Let's," he said.

"Now," Bill began, "remember the taxidermied cinghiale head from earlier?"

"Of course."

"Well, I have one problem with that, and it has nothing to do with the stuffing and mounting of animal heads."

"Let me guess," Jacoby said. "It has something to do with food."

"It does," Bill said. "And the food I'm talking about here is the cheek."

Jacoby poked a forefinger into the side of his face and twisted it.

"Yes," Bill said. "The cheek, or guancia in Italian."

"The Italian word sounds better," Jacoby declared.

"Agreed," said Bill. "And a more significant improvement, at least for gastronomic purposes, is the word guanciale, the cheek of our wild swines."

"And that word sounds like it would taste better than 'hog cheek." Jacoby said.

"Yes," Bill continued as the waiter put down a carafe of white wine and two glasses along with two menus. "Aspetta," Bill asked him to wait before he could walk away and then ordered quickly in Italian accompanied by hand gestures that resembled stylish sign language.

"I thought I was going to do the ordering," Jacoby complained when the waiter walked away.

"Not tonight," Bill said. "And not with any Italian asshole like him. You are permitted to avoid any attempts at communication with such types."

Jacoby thought of Helen's rather impassioned complaint about a certain type of bizarrely entitled Italian man, a few of whom he'd had up close encounters with already, including the malevolent hunter from Antella whom Jacoby quickly dashed from his thoughts. "Probably still lives at home with his mother," Jacoby joked about the waiter.

Bill laughed out loud and poured some white wine into their glasses. "Probably does," he said, still shuttering a bit from laughter. "Very clever."

"Thanks," Jacoby said, feeling very clever and taking a sip of refreshing wine with just enough depth to be interesting. "Oooh. I could drink this all day."

"Frascati," Bill said with a hand toward the room. "The primary wine of Lazio, and people do drink it all day."

"Tell me more about the cinghiale cheek."

Bill went on to explain how the cheeks of cinghiale are seasoned and cured into guanciale, then cut into match-stick shaped pieces and the unctuous fat rendered down into the base with the meat used to top the signature pasta dishes of Lazio: Carbonara, Gricia, and Amatriciana, as well as a few slight variations.

"Which ones are we having tonight?" Jacoby asked.

"Two of the three," Bill said, matter of fact. "Plus one lacking in any meat, Cacio e Pepe."

"Three courses?" Jacoby asked. "Are we tourists now?"

"Relax," Bill smiled. "It's a half plate of each, though that still is a lot of food. Or, at least, a lot of pasta. I just feel like it's important to root you in these plates on the first night, so we have a familiarity with each from day one."

Jacoby pumped his fists in mock dedication. "You have my full support."

"Good," Bill said, pouring more wine. "Of course, afterward, we will have to take a walk and enjoy a grappa for digestion purposes."

Jacoby put his hands in prayer in front of his chest and nodded as two half-plates of steaming Cacio e Pepe arrived.

· · ·

Jacoby liked the aesthetic already, long tubes of tonnarello aglow in a silky sheen of translucent sauce with grated white cheese and lots of cracked black pepper. The tang of the pepper tapped Jacoby's nose, backed by the pronounced yet mellow aroma of the cheese.

"Why no guanciale here?" Jacoby asked.

"Oh," Bill rose from his lurch forward to inhale the fragrance of the pasta. "Traditionalists leave meat out of this plate, leaving it to simply three ingredients: pasta, typically tonnarello like we have here, cheese, Pecorino Romano, of course, and black pepper."

"That's it?"

"That's it."

Jacoby twirled a long noodle and put it in his mouth. The flavors spread nicely: an earthy pop from the pepper and salt from the cheese working in concert with the toothy, perfectly coated pasta. Simple enough, but Jacoby had a question formulating as he swallowed, and Bill was ready for it.

"Pasta water," Bill said. He had been watching Jacoby eat and had yet to touch his plate.

Jacoby wiped his mouth with a cloth napkin. "What?"

"The creaminess comes from adding some of the pasta water, loaded with starch, once the noodles are combined with the sauce. It's one of the secrets of Cucina Romana."

"So many secrets," Jacoby joked. "So little time."

"I'll do my best to share as many of them as I can with you while we are here," Bill confirmed before tucking into his bowl of Cacio e Pepe.

The subsequent courses were equally impressive. The Carbonara featured the fresh strozzapreti and was a thicker version of the previous plate with a richness from the egg that pleased Jacoby's palate, and the crispy, salty, herb-informed nuggets of dark guanciale provided a vivid aesthetic contrast along with a burst of righteous flavor.

"Oy my god," Jacoby said. "That is so good."

"It's my favorite of all of them," Bill said. "One night I'll take you for the carbonara da sogno in all of Rome, where they will gild the lily to utter perfection."

Jacoby washed the feel of the sauce and the flavor of the guanciale from his mouth with Frescati and asked to know when and where they would take this meal.

"It will remain one of our secrets until then," Bill said.

The Amatriciana sauce over a traditional bucatini noodle brought some acid from the tomato-base and fresh herb in the form of basil.

The guanciale was evident in the sweet onions rendered in the drippings and in the nuggets dispersed throughout.

Jacoby found it interesting that the Frascati, the latter half of a second carafe, stood up to the tomato sauce, and he and Bill discussed this and other important matters about his introduction to Cucina Romana as they walked away from Campo de' Fiori to take a grappa at a quiet cafe off a cobbled side street.

Chapter 12

Campo de' Fiori was alive in the morning with a market that covered most of its cobblestone surface. Fresh air swirled among the cramped booths, shaded under canvas awnings, offering mostly fruits and vegetables from the nearby countryside but also dry goods and homewares and so many flowers. The colors and array dazzled Jacoby as he wandered and browsed steps behind Bill who walked slowly with his hands clasped behind him.

Prosaic moments like these, ones so viscerally life affirming, are what Jacoby cherished most about Italy. There was this perpetual sweet spot between invigorating and soothing that brought him great balance and comfort, such as this open market on a regular morning drenched in glorious sunshine that lifted his spirits and filled him with a joy that he could feel in his bones and sense on his skin. He trailed Bill like a happy puppy to an outdoor table of the bar where they had an aperitivo the night before.

Jacoby was experimenting with different coffee drinks, and he asked for a macchiato, an espresso with a dash of frothy steamed milk, while Bill enjoyed his daily cappuccino. They both fingered apart delicate strips of cornetti and savored the pieces of flaky pastry that dissolved in their mouths. Jacoby was dressed for walking in stylish Merrill sneakers, stretchy khaki slacks and a black V-neck T that clung comfortably to his slender frame. He had a pair of Ray Ban shades, but he held them most of the time, not wanting to be denied the vibrancy of Italy. His phone charged and a wallet full of Euros, his caffè and cornetto finished, it was time to prepare for the day.

Much to Jacoby's surprise, Bill did not present an ambitious itinerary or an overwhelming list of requirements. Or even a map. His advice was to "mingle with the city and listen to the people," while finding, in this order: Largo di Torre Argentina, the Pantheon, Fontana di Trevi, the Spanish Steps, lunch at Nino Ristorante, Piazza del Popolo, Villa Borghese Park (find the Galleria Borghese but don't enter) and then to return by the same route he came, stopping again at each site, to foster familiarity. He was also encouraged to step into every modest church to admire the serenity and artwork.

"But aren't there other sites I should see?" Jacoby asked with regard to his modest agenda.

"Yes," Bill said, "and you will see some of them, but this is not New York, Jacoby. Rome might not have been built in a day, but you can get somewhat familiar with it over the course of a few."

"Somewhat?" Jacoby asked and then immediately regretted it.

"Why, yes," Bill said, bemused. "You are not here to conquer the city. You are here to enjoy it. It takes weeks, months, years to get to know a place. And who knows, maybe you will return here again and again, but for now, our time is limited, so let's plan accordingly and make it meaningful. Let's think of this visit as a first date. Shall we?"

"OK," Jacoby agreed. "A first date. I like that."

"I thought you would," Bill said. "Now be off and meet me here at 4:00 to get you cleaned up and ready for a very special dinner."

Jacoby breathed in through his nose and let it out slowly.

. . .

Jacoby had tapped the information from Bill into his phone, and he held it by his side as he set off away from the piazza in the direction Bill had instructed. The sun was shining, and the air was the perfect temperature that made no impression on the skin. The city pulsed with pedestrians and vehicles, but it was not crowded. Jacoby coveted distance between strangers, not miles, just six feet or so, where you didn't have to be privy to really anything beyond the look of their face.

Riding packed New York City subways during rush hour was among the things he missed least about America.

The wide road that had brought them from the Wedding Cake building was teeming with traffic and the urban energy of commuting. As the sounds of the vehicles whipped past, Jacoby acknowledged the blessing of his freedom, to be on unexpected holiday in Rome, under the guidance of a expert, as he stepped off the sidewalk, across a small square with a fountain, and up a few steps into the cool confines of the magnificent basilica of Sant'Andrea della Valle. Incense lingered in the cool, shaded air from an early morning service. The entire interior felt like a museum with frescoes and sculptures and framed paintings among the chapels and marble and a minor dome.

He didn't stay long and was upon Largo di Torre Argentina before the sun could warm his face and forearms. The sunken square in a wide clearing featured many columns in ruin, umbrella pines and a colony of feral cats. Jacoby turned the circumference once around and found a sign for the Pantheon, which directed him down a narrow, shaded street of smooth, blue cobblestones. Many of the shops opened to the street, and Jacoby admired the products, especially those with food on display, but vowed to abstain from eating until the restaurant Bill recommended for lunch. He did take water from a cracked fountain and noted its clear taste.

The quaint lane was lined with facades of pastel colors and windows with open shutters, plant or flower boxes on the sills, occasional strings of ivy dangling overhead between the buildings. In Rome, Jacoby recognized, plants and flowers were everywhere, and that, in conjunction with the color scheme and low-slung layout, explained the sense of eternity. Rome would go on forever, Jacoby thought, as he began to fall in love with another Italian city.

The area around the Pantheon featured street life of Rome. A guitarist with an amplified acoustic sang for tips by a fountain with an obelisk that fronted the church. There were tour groups gathered and horse-pulled carriages waiting for fares. Dark immigrants performed or begged, many of the latter women and children in such desperate physical condition that Jacoby felt both horror and sorrow. He gave a woman in a full body garment, on her knees with her head down and a cup in the air, 20 Euros in an effort to somewhat help them both.

Jacoby passed through the towering yet pocked columns of the Pantheon, reminded of the sadness that existed, even among the splendor, of the world's cities and the world itself. Past the portico and through massive bronze doors was a wide hall that could not redeem the world's suffering but exhilarated Jacoby nonetheless. Above the pristine marbled walls and columns of faint shade, adorned with ornate tombs and panels and art, was a massive dome with a perfect circle opening. Jacoby stood directly below, on top of the draining holes that collect the rainwater, and stared up at a shaft of light that slanted through. There was something in the light, but he didn't know what it was. Jacoby stared until his neck hurt and then wandered outside without direction, unsure of his thoughts until his senses returned and he realized he was lost.

"Mi scusi," Jacoby asked a well-heeled woman clicking past.

The woman stopped, tilted her head and smiled. "Sì?"

"Quale direzione è la Fontana di Trevi?"

"Avanti," she said with a flick of her wrist.

"Vicino?" Jacoby asked if it was close, mostly just to ask.

"Molto vicino," she said. "Pochi passi."

Jacoby made a praying gesture with his hands. "Grazie," he said.

"Prego," the woman responded with a nod and walked off, her heels somehow navigating the shifted cobblestones.

Jacoby pulled out his phone and made a voice memo: Pochi passi. He would ask Bill later what it exactly meant, though he had a good idea.

Following yet another narrow lane, lined with quaint shops beneath pastel walls strewn with flowers and plants, brought Jacoby - a few blocks after crossing a busy thoroughfare - within earshot of cascading water and the murmur of a crowd. And with the turn of a corner, among the increase in volume, was an enormous display of statues, a theater, really, fronted by huge basins of rushing water, erupting from the facade of a palace. "Oh my god," Jacoby said, feeling mesmerized once again in Italy, as if he were still a child.

The sculpture and pools extended over the entire width of the palace, with passages for walking on three sides. The front side had an open space for gathering and best access to the large pool and the mind boggling backdrop. Tourists filled the landing, marveling and taking pictures and throwing coins over their shoulders into the emerald-tinged water that sparkled at the basin's bottom a few feet below. The dramatic sculpture, set upon staggered rock formations dripping with falling water, featured an ensemble of gods and mermaids and beasts with, as always, some bravo dude with six-pack abs, barely dressed, flowing hair, front and center.

Jacoby loved this stuff, but he didn't take part in the rituals or even take any pictures. He didn't even desire to read any of the explanations about who the figures were or what was symbolized. He'd, perhaps, find out during other visits. He preferred at first or even second glance to just admire the magnificence and take comfort and inspiration, as he did in the other marvels of Italy, in the accomplishments of man. Just the fact that human beings conceived this and built it hundreds of years ago was enough for him. Besides, he was getting hungry.

He noted a sign for the Spanish Steps on his way over the busy road, so he retraced his steps and followed the posh, active two-way past the swanky shops of elite national and international brands. The wide, for Rome, sidewalks were crowded with shoppers; the road busy in both directions with the full parade of Roman vehicles, including double-decker buses used for tours. Bill had mentioned a bus tour at one point, but Jacoby thought he was joking. Seeing the city on foot was clearly the only way to go.

Said feet started to ache in the arch as he followed signs from the Spanish Steps that kept him for lengthy stretches on streets bordered with shiny storefronts between the rushing traffic. When Jacoby arrived at the Spanish Steps - a towering, spreading expanse - he did the obvious and felt his breath increase as he trudged toward the landing that fronted the facade of another magnificent church.

Jacoby arrived at the Piazza Trinità dei Monti, sweaty around the neck and dry in his throat, his dark hair holding heat on the top of his head, his fingers and feet a little puffy. He leaned into the alabaster balustrade and looked straight across the rooftops with some cupolas in the distance backed by a billowing tree line. The sky was a perfect blue sheet. The immediate buildings, split by a narrow street, showcased the pastels and roof tiles and gardens that best defined the prosaic Roman architecture that belied Jacoby's original expectation of Rome being more chaos than charm. He breathed through his nose and smelled flowers. And food.

After an expedited tour of the Trinità dei Monti church, Jacoby descended the steep staircase as the enormous bell towers began to bong 12 times. He crossed Piazza di Spagna in search of his lunch destination, Nino Ristorante, which he found a mere one block away - thanks to Google Maps and the name of the restaurant in large vertical letters extended above the entrance. The inside was cool and not crowded, white tablecloths and dark wainscoting that matched the chairs. The waiters were dressed nicely and impeccably polite. The faint sound of an opera could be heard. Jacoby thought it might be too fancy, especially in his sweat-cloaked t-shirt, but he was made to feel welcome and seated at a private table with room on all sides and lovely artwork on the walls. Lunch time.

Chapter 13

When Jacoby returned from the washroom, a menu awaited along with the frizzante water he had requested. Upon first glance of the menu, Jacoby was somewhat taken back by the fact that the cuisine was dedicated to Tuscan food since he was in Rome and lived in Tuscany - after all, wasn't that the point of cucina tipica - but closer inspection revealed a distinct Roman influence. He thought of Bill's intentions and sleight of hand. A wink from a fellow traveler. Funny. Jacoby avoided the Tuscan staples and took fried artichokes for a starter accompanied by the house white which he recognized immediately as a crisp, cold Frascati that effectively followed the earth and salt and crunch of the flower buds. For the second course, Jacoby was thinking meat after all that pasta the night before, but none of the Roman cuts were familiar, so he winged it and ordered the "cervello" having no idea what that was but feeling lucky if not a bit cocky.

The waiter nodded with a look of approval, and Jacoby felt a little electric and sophisticated sitting alone in a Roman ristorante, the taste of fried artichoke lingering and a waiter not only understanding his Italian but impressed by his order.

"Con burro o fritto?" the waiter asked.

Jacoby's confidence expanded, knowing precisely what was being asked, even if he was still unsure, and leery to ask, of what would be cooked in butter or fried.

"Burro, per favore," Jacoby answered, already having had a plate of fried food.

The waiter nodded with even more enthusiasm and went off with the order as Jacoby sat back and crossed his legs, sipping some sparkling water and unsuccessfully eavesdropped on a nearby conversation between two handsome middle-aged men in custom-made suits. He thought that they may have been lawyers by the way they bantered more than talked. And that might explain why the language was so out of context. He made a point to sit next to Italian families or young people whenever possible. Jacoby casually put his cell phone on the table and activated the Voice Memo feature. He would try to translate later at his pace, with Bill's help, though he kept listening intently and didn't take notice when the waiter put a silver spoon at his place setting, though it should have been a hint that his confidence in his order was misplaced.

The "cervello" arrived on a dish under a silver plated cover. The only aromas were of butter and sage and garlic, so he was still unsure of what the meat would be until the waiter whisked off the cover. Then he knew. And there it was, just like in a laboratory: a brain. He thought of that one Indiana Jones movie where monkey brain was the main course.

"Che cos'è?" Jacoby asked what it was.

"Cervello," the waiter answered as if it was obvious.

"Io so," Jacoby recognized. "Cervello di cosa?"

"Agnello," the waiter answered.

"Grazie," Jacoby said, thankful the brain was of, at least, a lamb.

He picked up the spoon and was mad at himself for not taking notice earlier and asking about the spoon's purpose, instead of a sharp knife, for a meat dish. He might have been able to cancel the order before it was too late. But it was too late now. He would feel like a fool and a fraud if he sent it back, so he dug in. And it sounded worse than it looked, a sucking, squishy sound as the membrane parted and butter seeped into the gap. The aroma of the organ escaped the aromatics as the bite got close to his mouth. The texture caused his stomach to flip over on itself and his shoulders to hunch towards his mouth, as if trying to reject the normal digestive process. He suppressed, best he could, the gagging reflex in the back of his throat. The mouth-feel reminded him of the raw sausage he had eaten for breakfast in the back of the village butcher shop in Antella, but this was worse. Way worse, as it had a more slippery than tacky feel. More gelatinous. And he couldn't squeegee it off his tongue with his teeth. Or ring the flavor from his mouth. After swallowing, and ignoring any attempt to identify flavor, he washed his mouth, as best he could without swishing, with a gulp of frizzante, which he chased with the last of the Frascati.

Jacoby took a deep breath and looked down at his lunch. He figured he could get away with eating half and still save face. Of course, it would be worse if he puked all over the table. Sweat pricks streaked across his forehead and chills climbed up his spine. He took another bite and then put the spoon down as the waiter arrived to check on him.

Jacoby put a hand to his chest in a gesture of confession. "Mi dispiace," he said. "Io non so la significanza di cervello."

"It's OK," the waiter said in English, adding insult to injury. "It happen."

The waiter took the plate and held up a hand in consolation before walking away. Jacoby stewed in his own humiliation, complicated by the fact that he was still hungry, even after the two most disgusting bites of his life. Considering the check and a quick escape, Jacoby looked up as the waiter returned.

"Would you like something else?" the waiter asked.

Jacoby sat up, determined. "Sì," he said confidently and then asked the waiter in Italian, first, for them to speak only in Italian, and then for him to choose a vegetable dish to complete the lunch.

The waiter smiled kindly and nodded. "D'accordo," he agreed.

·　　·　　·

Jacoby returned to the spangling sunshine of Rome after lunch feeling accomplished, despite the humiliation and horror. The waiter chose a satisfying timballo of roasted zucchini bright with tomato sauce and aromatics, fortified with rice and grated cheese, that paired nicely with the house red. They didn't charge him for the brain, which Jacoby felt badly about but appreciated nonetheless. And he learned a new word in Italian, though he vowed to never utter 'cervello' again.

The walk from Piazza di Spagna to Piazza del Popolo was fairly quick and, once again, within the confines of a high rent district. Lots of fabulous on display, and Jacoby could imagine Dolores having a high time bouncing from shop to shop. Italian fashion was a curiosity to Jacoby, from the elegant to the absurd, and always fun to observe. Beyond the miracle women routinely performed of effortlessly navigating the streets - often on shifted cobblestones with gaps between them - on shoes with high and skinny heels, he found men's fashion to be far more interesting. There was an odd combination of macho and effete, of baffling patterns that he could never imagine seeing in a store and deciding to buy. There also seemed to be no limits on how many buttons on a button down shirt that go unfastened.

Being immersed in another culture was not only fascinating but invigorating, and Jacoby recognized the affirmation of this on a regular basis and wondered if this was the evergreen experience of an expat, of fascination in exchange for the comfort of familiarity. And Jacoby's fascination was conjured upon his arrival at Piazza del Popolo, a massive square, circular in shape, with a towering obelisk in the center and twin, modest churches with matching columns and cupolas among the edifices of the perimeter, where there were also enough statues to fill a museum wing. Jacoby crossed the cobblestones and sat on the steps around the obelisk as pigeons pecked and flocked. A young couple was breaking up with great passion, and Jacoby couldn't stand to eavesdrop on their pain, so he walked toward the treeline that had to be the Villa Borghese gardens.

The road from which he entered the gardens was wide and cool under a canopy of umbrella pines. The landscaped grounds held their lush summer greenery. Lakes and ponds featured the iridescent green found in the larger fountains within the city. Joggers and bicyclists flitted past; tourists covered the paths on bikes and golf carts and paddle cars. There was even a tour with those Segway things Jacoby found so annoying. He preferred walking, and walk he did through the peaceful surroundings, wishing the whole time that he was back on the streets. Jacoby didn't mind nature, but urban parks such as this, their importance acknowledged for denizens, lacked the energy he loved when exploring a city. The parks were an oasis, but he didn't want an escape. He was reminded here, somewhat, of the Commons in Boston in the tranquility. In fact, Rome, with its emphasis on history, size and relative navigability, reminded Jacoby a lot of Boston, though "history" in this sense, was relative to the point of absurdity.

Along the gravel paths, Jacoby listened to the birds high up in the trees and enjoyed the slotted sunshine that penetrated the cover in golden bands. The Galleria Borghese was a pull, and Jacoby took a long drink from a fountain by a garden of manicured hedges. There were groups gathered out front of the austere, modest villa in a shade of white. He could hear one of the tour guides talking in English about tickets and their time of entry, so he now realized why he was instructed by Bill not to enter, though he was still unsure of why he had to come this far in the first place.

He took a picture of the museum and texted it to Helen, asking if she'd ever been.

"Of course, you dolt," she responded almost immediately and then asked, "On a scale of 10 through 10, how much do you miss me?"

Jacoby responded "11" and began his walk back to Campo de' Fiori, per Bill's instructions, following the exact same route he had taken.

Chapter 14

Jacoby walked with less urgency on the way home, wandering somewhat, observing more and experiencing a different pace. He recognized the reason, here as well, for Bill's instruction: to reemphasize the known, not experience the new. In this spirit, Jacoby, after climbing the Spanish Steps for a second time and passing through Piazza di Spagna, took his familiar gelato combo of pistacchio and stracciatella from a street side shop on Via dei Condotti, the separate flavors of pistacchio and vanilla with chocolate chips still seducing him with every small spoonful.

The energy of Via del Corso, even during the quiet afternoon hours dedicated to rest, swept him along, and he was grateful to detour and stroll the side street that led to the Fontana di Trevi. The crowd had increased since earlier, and Jacoby acknowledged that there are some sites in Rome which know no reprieve from tourists. Made sense. The fountain had the overwhelming impact of certain Italian treasures, one that stole breath and thumped the chest and inspired marvel, even during repeat visits. Jacoby thought of "David" in Florence and the evergreen impact when approaching that masterpiece.

After a second pass through the Pantheon, Jacoby veered off route to do a little discovering and get another look at the Wedding Cake building. He was down with the philosophy of second helpings, but he had plenty of time before meeting Bill, and he had a sense of where he was. In the vicinity of the Piazza Venezia were grand palaces and a heavy military presence, serious men in stylish uniforms, standing in front of elaborate vestibules or sitting in jeeps parked askance, with assault weapons at the ready. Jacoby assumed they were there to guard the residences of royalty, politicians or fashion designers.

On his way toward Largo di Torre Argentina, Jacoby entered another magnificent church off of the busy Corso Vittorio Emanuele II, the road Jacoby recognized as taken by the cab (was it just yesterday?) from the train station to Campo de' Fiori and that he had also walked, from the opposite direction, in the morning. He also noted that the name of the major thoroughfare or "corso" was that of the king who had unified Italy in the late 1800s. The learning process empowered him, but he was quick to remind himself of the pacing required of Bill's pedagogy.

Jacoby sat in the last pew of the main chapel, breathing the remnants of incense from an afternoon service and watching the elaborately dressed clergy clearing the sanctuary of their rituals. Jacoby wondered what kind of wine they drank; and then he felt badly for thinking of that. And then he wondered again. It had to be good. He protected himself from a potential bolt of lightning for his blasphemous thoughts by studying the spectacular decor throughout the church, particularly the arched roof covered in a colorful fresco. And then he laughed. A mirror was strategically placed at the back of the nave, tilted to allow for a photo that would include the visitor and the ceiling. He waited for someone to confirm his suspicion before taking his own selfie, a practice Jacoby detested but figured was OK in this case, apparently approved of and encouraged by God.

Sitting on the steps outside the church, Jacoby texted the photo to Helen with his "God approved" interpretation. He mingled with the cats among the ruined towers and other structures of Largo di Torre Argentina before passing the church he had entered first thing that morning. The adventure felt complete and successful, his spirit uplifted by the experience of travel and discovery, especially in Italy, where he would soon meet his dear friend for an aperitivo, get cleaned up and dressed nicely, then go out for what would surely be an incredible, wine-soaked dinner in the Italian capital of Rome.

. . .

The Campo de' Fiori was busy with the end of the open air market. Small vehicles or carts were loaded with products and stands were dismantled. Clean up crews swept and gathered garbage; the cobblestones were hosed down. Activity around the perimeter was meager, and the outdoor seating area of the bar was shaded and empty except for Bill, who sat still as a statue, a leg crossed over the other and his arms folded over his chest. Jacoby recognized one of Bill's postures for repose and marveled at his ability to nap almost anywhere. He's going to live to 100, Jacoby thought happily and with great optimism until the thought of his friend's lonely heart saddened him.

"Hey," Jacoby said, sitting down.

Bill opened his eyes and spoke without pause. "Oh, hello Jacoby. How was your day?"

Jacoby shrugged, bunched up his face and tilted a flat hand from side to side. "Così così," he said, using one of his favorite expressions, enhanced, he thought, by sarcasm.

"Oh," Bill said with a wan smile. "I will do my best to make tomorrow less average."

Jacoby shook Bill's shoulder playfully, and Bill's eyes sparkled when he smiled. "How did you do today?" Jacoby asked, reading his friend's high spirits.

"Quite well," Bill said, "by Italian standards."

The waitress approached and Jacoby ordered two Aperol Spritzes without hesitation before turning his eyes back to Bill. "What's that mean?"

"It means that progress was made, but we will be here for at least a few more days."

"Works for me," Jacoby said as a young nun pedaled past on a bicycle.

"I imagine," Bill said with a wry tone. "I'll try to keep you from being too bored."

The two men sat without speaking as the expanse slowly emptied like the dismantling of a puzzle. Jacoby thought of rhythm and routine, the day in, day out that Italians had mastered in a manner that felt extraordinary. Their drinks arrived, and the happy expats nodded to each other, as if in on a secret to life, and raised their glasses in toast to their health.

The bitter and cold and fizz felt good in Jacoby's mouth and pleased his palate. He enjoyed medicinal flavor up front and the dry finish from the prosecco. The swelling from excessive walking began to leave his hands. The sun tilted down and the evening cool swept in from the side streets. Someone began to play an accordion on the far side of the piazza, near the fountain where some teens in school uniforms had gathered. People began to pass on their way home from work. Pigeons pecked at edibles from the market gathered in the cracks between the cobblestones. Jacoby told Bill about his encounter with the lamb's brain, and Bill found the story as amusing as anything he'd heard in a very long time.

Chapter 15

They crossed the square as the burnished light of dusk sifted down, both men clean and sharp, ready for dinner out, in shirts and slacks, loafers and leather belts. Jacoby was hungry, and Bill was excited, his cheeks pink and his eyes sparkling, his pace quicker than the Italians who strolled in the last remnants of the magic hour. Warm lights glowed and quick, fragrant breezes spun around the open expanse. A breeze lifted Jacoby's collar and reminded him of something he wanted to ask Bill.

"Are we near the sea?" he asked.

"Why, yes," Bill stopped to answer. "Why do you ask?"

"I don't know," Jacoby shrugged. "I never thought of Rome as being near the ocean, but I've been smelling it at times, just hints, since we stepped outside the train station."

Bill laughed and took Jacoby by the shoulders. "What did our dear Ms. Claire used to say about you?"

"Before she broke off our engagement or after?" Jacoby answered with an intentionally sheepish smirk.

"I'm guessing it was before and after," Bill answered relaxing his hands down. "But the only time I heard her mention it was at our celebratory meal after the auction, when we were talking about what a marvelous palate you have."

"Oh," Jacoby laughed. "That. Yeah. She used to call me an 'olfactory genius.'"

"Yes," Bill said. "That's exactly it. And she was correct."

Bill continued their walk and exited the square on a side street with its cobblestones cloaked in pale light.

"So I was right," Jacoby confirmed after sidling back up to Bill. "The ocean is nearby."

"It is," Bill confirmed. "But don't tell anyone. It is one of Rome's best kept secrets."

"I promise," Jacoby agreed before asking. "Got any more secrets to share?"

"Why, yes," Bill acknowledged. "In fact, we are on our way to one of the very best right now, a trattoria perfectly suited for an olfactory genius."

Jacoby rubbed his hands together as they walked. "Nice. I hope it's close," he said before repeating his favorite Italian expression, that of being hungry. "Ho fame."

"Good," Bill said. "And it is close. In fact, we're almost there."

• • •

After a few quick turns, not 200 yards beyond the square, down boutique-lined lanes busy with pedestrians, a restaurant was tucked, a few storefronts down from the corner, beyond a closed bar, nearly into the darkness of a silent street. The small space for dining out front was empty, the tables pushed together and not set.

"Wait here," Bill advised and went inside the nearly empty and modest interior aglow in soft light.

In the shimmering silence, Jacoby watched stars appear in the darkening sky until Bill returned, bantering in Italian with a young waitress who greeted Jacoby with a friendly "Ciao" and began to assemble a table for two.

"Everything OK?" Jacoby asked, thinking Bill's secret had, perhaps, lost its magic in his long absence.

"Yes. Yes," he said. "I just thought it would be nice to eat outside while we still had the chance."

"Prego," the waitress said to Jacoby, motioning with her hand toward a readied place setting.

"Grazie," Jacoby responded and sat down, his back to the arched entrance of a residence above the restaurant and his eyes on the narrow street of cobblestones, bordered by a faded wall of orange with closed shutters and a small doorway where a cat, circled into itself, slept in a basket. He thought of Boy and assured himself that Nicoletta and Giovanni were taking good care of him. Still, he missed his dog.

Bill joined Jacoby after the waitress assembled his place and returned inside, surely, Jacoby thought, to return soon with some wine. Through the glass facade, he watched her cross the room past a cluster of unoccupied waitstaff.

"I guess your secret is still safe," Jacoby said.

"Very funny," Bill responded. "It is early and the off-season."

"True," Jacoby acknowledged with a nod.

"And, of course, the maestro has yet to arrive."

"Who?"

"Chef Livio," Bill said and then motioned with his head over Jacoby's shoulder.

A light came on above the doorway, and a small commotion bound down the stairs. When the noise reached the landing, the door opened, and a large man in a white chef's uniform appeared. He had wild, raven hair and a matching beard, his thick hands, held up as if in worship, were adorned on every finger with silver rings. His eyes were wide and his mouth turned up within the thick growth. He looked, to Jacoby, more like a pirate than a chef.

"Vieni qui," he ordered Bill, in a voice both deep and strange, to come to him.

Bill obliged without pause. Under the fake light, the two men hugged, Bill's entire upper body nearly disappearing into the massive chef's coat. Livio rocked Bill back and forth with both joy and comfort. Jacoby recognized that Livio and Bill must have shared a bond, also, as strangers in Italy, which explained his appearance and accent.

Livio eventually released Bill. Jacoby was properly introduced and thoroughly impressed by the warmth and bravado that emanated from this man of abundance. Livio spoke with great enthusiasm to both men, with flailing hands in a dialect of Italian unrecognizable to Jacoby, though he could gather that Livio was happy they were there and making great promises. When the maestro stormed inside the restaurant, the staff burst into movement. Bill and Jacoby sat down.

"Wow," Jacoby marveled.

"Yes," Bill agreed. "He's quite a character."

"I'll say."

"And, as expected, he has promised a meal not to be forgotten."

"What's it going to be?" Jacoby asked with relish.

"We will just have to wait and see," Bill responded.

They didn't have to wait long. A few expat couples and some groups of hip, young Italians met outside to smoke and chat before entering, causing the formerly quiet enclave to come to life as the waitress set up an ice bucket between Bill and Jacoby and filled it with two bottles of white and one of red.

"Oh, boy," Jacoby noted.

"Yes," Bill sighed. "It's going to be one of those evenings."

Jacoby pulled the bottle of red from its icy depths and studied the label.

Bill responded without having to be asked. "It's Romanian."

"Really?"

"Yes, they make wonderful wines there, very big reds. The cooling tempers them somewhat. I imagine it will come out of the ice during the previous course of which it will accompany."

"And what will that be?"

"I have a suspicion, a strong one," Bill answered, "but I'm going to let it be a surprise as Livio enjoys the theatrics."

"Is that where he's from?" Jacoby asked. "Romania?"

"Why, yes," Bill said, not bothering to compliment Jacoby for being clever. "They actually have a wonderful cuisine there, very Mediterranean with accents from the East."

A young waiter with long hair and tattoos on his hands and forearms brought a cutting board covered in grilled and roasted vegetables and soft cheese. The colors were vibrant and familiar.

"The Italian flag," Jacoby observed, taking note of the tri-colors of red, green, and white on display. He helped himself to a plate of roasted red peppers, grilled zucchini, and burrata. Bill did the same.

While they were eating, a different server arrived with two small plates, each with grilled langoustines, their shells bright pink, on a gelatinous sheen of glowing yellow sauce.

"What is that?" Jacoby asked.

Bill shook his head, dipped a finger tip in the sauce and brought it to his mouth. He stared at the end of his nose for a moment, opened and closed his mouth a few times to agitate his tongue, and then looked without expression at Jacoby. He shook his head again and motioned with deference for Jacoby to give it a shot.

The so-called 'olfactory genius' accepted the challenge. He sipped some wine to cleanse his palate and then removed a tail from a langoustine shell and dipped it in the sauce. The contrast in flavor from the briny shellfish brought out the egg yolk and lemon and dry wine of the sauce. At the finish was a hint of saffron. Jacoby identified the flavors but didn't know the name of the sauce or how it was so vibrant in color.

"We will have to ask Livio later," Bill said, impressed by Jacoby's deciphering of flavors.

When the langoustines were finished, a platter of fried mounds arrived that Jacoby thought he recognized from American pizzerias.

"Rice balls?" he asked.

"Ah, not quite," Bill said. "In Italy there are variations, the best known are arancini in the south and supplì al telefono here in Rome. Obviously, the version indigenous to here is the best."

"Obviously," Jacoby agreed, recognizing the importance of provincialism to Italian culture.

"Though here, under the auspices of Livio, we get a version inspired by his homeland, made from polenta instead of rice and filled with, what I suspect will be, both cheese and meat.

Jacoby was already biting one before Bill finished his sentence. "Yep," he said through a full mouth, bursting with salt and tang amid the crunchy outer texture. He kept his mouth open and panted to allow the heat to escape until he was ready to swallow and proclaim, "So good."

Bill split his croquette in half, blew on the open face and took a small bite. "Do you taste the pieces of pork belly?"

"Un-huh," Jacoby muttered, savoring another bite. "Killing me here."

"And the feta cheese?"

"Mmm-hmm," Jacoby confirmed. "There's sour cream, too."

"That makes sense," Bill nodded. "These are inspired by Mamaliga, the national dish of Romania, of which sour cream is an important component."

Jacoby disappeared into another croquette and identified the subtle herb as parsley, offering moisture and texture more than flavor.

The second white, an Orvieto from Umbria, was a little rounder and more crisp than the Frascati with which they started. The Orvieto stood up nicely to the complex croquette, all fried and savory and creamy, spiked with seasonings. Jacoby cleansed his palate and let the layers of the wine settle on his tongue. He interlaced his fingers and sat back in his chair as Bill conversed joyfully with a server removing their plates.

The moon rose above the roof line, round and white as a porcelain plate. Stillness settled as everything outside the trattoria was cloaked in a silver veil. God, how Jacoby loved such moments. Being with a friend out front of a Roman restaurant, indulging in exquisite food and washing it down with perfect wines just seemed like the most important place in all of the world. Or, in less grandiose terms: It felt so human. So simple yet special. And isn't that how life was supposed to be? That intersection of the profound and the prosaic that validated the beauty of being alive. Italy allowed that like no other place he'd ever been. No wonder he was so happy. And no wonder his happiness came so naturally, without conditions or complications.

Jacoby's heady contemplation and emotional indulgence was interrupted by a small crew of servers who began to set up an outdoor grilling station built into a stone precipice on the far side of the courtyard. A crackling sound commenced and wood smoke rose towards the cornices of the low buildings that bordered the silent street. Jacoby smelled pine. A waitress pulled the bottle of red from the bucket, popped the cork and left it on the table to breathe and release some of the chill.

"As I suspected," Bill said with a confident wrinkle of his lips.

"The next course?" Jacoby asked.

"Exactly," Bill said then sipped some of the remaining white wine.

"Are you gonna tell me?" Jacoby asked with mock-exasperation.

"Take a look for yourself," he instructed as a waiter walked past with a platter stacked with long bones scraped free of sinew; the round loins glistening ruby red with a thin layer of fat around the periphery. A hint of gaminess poked Jacoby's nose.

"Lamb chops," he said.

"A Roman specialty," Bill confirmed. "Right off the grill, eaten by hand, hence the name: Scottadito."

Jacoby wrinkled his brow and squinted.

"Burn the finger," Bill put him out of his monolingual misery and shook his hand to pantomime pain. "Scotta, to burn; dito, the finger."

"Love it," Jacoby said. "How long till they're ready?"

"Oh, not long," Bill said. "That's part of the beauty. The limited ingredients and quick cooking time."

"I'll be fast," Jacoby rose from his seat, dashing his idea to bum a smoke from a server and opt for the more important restroom visit instead.

Inside was busy with the orchestra of a restaurant: the chorus of chatter and silverware on plate surfaces and the cacophony from the kitchen; the dance of patrons and staff. The modest room featured muted colors and modern decor. Dispirit aromas mingled. Passing the open door of the kitchen, Jacoby spotted Livio posing for pictures with Italian hipsters, his big arm clutching each around the shoulder for the social media shot, a giant smile on his giant face. It made Jacoby think of how food people were so often happy people. Those who loved the planting and farming and harvesting, the procuring and preparing and sharing were among the people he knew to be the most well off in ways emotional and physical. What mattered more in life than being well? What would one trade for that?

Jacoby returned to the table as the mountain of Scottadito arrived, the original red meat and scraped bones now charred and flame licked.

The smell fired Jacoby's nose and sluiced his mouth with carnivorous splendor.

"Perfect timing," Bill recognized as red wine was poured into bulbous glasses.

The platter between the two men was arranged with the bones up in a tangled crown, juice glistening lightly from the loins gathered at the bottom of the platter. The aroma of tamed gaminess overwhelmed Jacoby, but he didn't want to be rude.

"Let's eat these while they're hot," Bill said with savor.

Jacoby reached for a chop, but Bill smacked his hand. "Aspetta," he told Jacoby to wait as he squeezed lemons over top, sprinkled them with coarse salt and stripped two rosemary twigs of their leaves.

Jacoby, a tad more calm, hoping to reestablish decorum and contemplating what appeared to be enough food for four, asked, "Is anyone else joining us?"

"God I hope not," Bill joked, before adding. "And you will be surprised how many of these beauties two meat enthusiasts can go through."

Jacoby swirled his wine glass and held it to his nose, recognizing the aging in oak and forward cherry aroma with some spice on the finish. Jacoby feared it would be a high alcohol, fruit bomb, like they make in California. He was pleased with the prospects of how it would pair with the lamb. He put the glass down and grabbed the first of what would be more than a dozen single chops of humanely raised, grass fed lamb that filled his mouth with song and his heart with content, enhanced by sips of the perfectly paired wine.

Bill and Jacoby went chop for chop and sip for sip until the lamb and wine were gone, gnawing the bones clean of any remnants of meat. They only managed to eat half the platter of roasted potatoes that arrived after the lamb, though the potatoes - as Jacoby learned, another Roman staple - were spectacular: crispy on the outside, soft and warm inside, seasoned with salt and rosemary and a sprinkle of Pecorino cheese. Jacoby wanted to take them home, but he knew that Italians didn't do that. He understood, but, damn, they would make a great breakfast whipped up with some eggs.

Livio came out as if to smoke but clearly wanted to check on the results of his feast. Bill rose slowly and gave him a cathartic and heartfelt hug. Jacoby also stood to thank the maestro, offering compliments through the most basic Italian and every gesture he could conjure to verify the taking of an epic meal. Livio smiled and sat his full body into the metal chair and threw his smokes on the table. Jacoby gestured toward the pack.

"Prego," Livio said. "Prego."

Jacoby slipped an American Spirit from the yellow pack and lit it from a small candle on a nearby table. He excused himself and walked toward the quiet corner where he leaned back, buttressed by the bottom of a foot, against an ancient wall under a cascade of dangling ivy illuminated by a wrought iron street lamp. Jacoby hadn't smoked much since Claire left and the packs she left in the barn disappeared, especially since Helen detested the practice, but on certain occasions - always having to do with a great meal - he enjoyed the physical act and the modest inhales he took, gathering the smoke in his mouth and throat, tasting the tobacco on exhale while watching it rise and drift away, in this case towards a dark sky rung with Roman stars.

Back at the table, Bill was crying. Livio comforted him with a hand on his forearm.

"What happened?" Jacoby asked, walking quickly up to Bill.

Livio began to answer, but Bill waved him off. "Oh, you know, Jacoby," he said, slightly embarrassed but regaining his composure. "Just a little reminiscing among all these memories just sets off the waterworks. Food especially does the trick, and the memories from Livio's food are almost too much to bare."

Livio said in broken English, "My lamb chop make him cry."

They all laughed. Jacoby rubbed Bill's back gently and resumed his seat. Bill sniffed and wiped his eyes with a cloth napkin. The ambiance from inside the restaurant spilled out and surrounded them with gentle sound. Jacoby studied Bill whose face was still furrowed with lingering pain.

"Want to rub some grappa on it?" Jacoby asked.

Bill laughed through his nose and rocked forward. "What a wonderful idea."

Livio howled and smacked the table. He yelled to a passing waiter who nodded and hurried on his way inside. The three men sat contently until the bottle of grappa arrived with three glasses. Jacoby poured, and they toasted to health. While Jacoby was relieved Bill was in better spirits, he was reminded of his own episodes of sensory memory: that of his mother, conjured by baking cookies, which always made him cry.

Chapter 16

In the morning, Jacoby was less hungover than he feared. The strain in his temple and the sour taste in his mouth was attributed more to the additional smokes he bummed off Livio as they worked their way through the bottle of grappa until Bill, wisely, put an end to their bender in the making. Still, Jacoby marveled at how two men could eat all that food and drink all that wine, finish with grappa, and still be functional. It was primarily a matter of pacing (the meal did take many hours) and the steady consumption of water throughout, but mostly it was the quality of the ingredients, the wine being devoid of sulfites and from grapes grown with minimal, if any, interference from chemicals; the food was all local, raised and produced with quality foremost in mind, not profit.

Bill, at 75 years old, indulged as thoroughly as Jacoby, a man more than 40 years his junior, and strolled home from the trattoria without the slightest stumble. He was up, once again, at the break of dawn for his morning walk. He looked sprightly and refreshed when Jacoby met him at the bar on the far end of the Campo for breakfast of a cornetto and caffè. Jacoby took a cornetto filled with a marmalade of pear, and he savored the sweetness contrasted with the flaky pastry. He went Americano for his coffee to cut through the fruit and sugar and dough.

Thin streaks of clouds stretched across the skyline, and moisture evaporated from the dew that had settled overnight. Jacoby smelled leaves aging in the clear, crisp morning air, and he could sense the season changing. He was dressed casually again, fresh T-shirt, stretch jeans and stylish sneakers. Bill dictated an itinerary that would take Jacoby in the opposite direction, complete with specific destinations and a recommendation for lunch that even included what to order. Jacoby didn't mind; there were few things he trusted more than the judgment and taste of his new friend, though it had occurred to Jacoby at some point that Bill was more of an old friend than a new one, despite only having known each other for four months. Jacoby was aware of how often he came back to this thought of his friendship with Bill, not just the thought itself but its recurring nature. There was something to that, but he wasn't sure what it was.

Bill strolled off toward an administrative district and Jacoby backtracked through the Campo as the market came to life. He veered off a side street by their residence to cross Corso Vittorio Emanuele II and access, within a few narrow streets, Piazza Navona, the size and shape of a football field with three elaborate fountains evenly spaced down the middle, a sturdy obelisk sprouting from the largest fountain in the expanse's center. The deep blue cobblestones were smooth and clean. Around the perimeter, baroque facades fronted the larger, more officious buildings while the familiar pastel residences had terraces and greenery with many cafes and eateries on the ground level featuring canopied, al fresco seating. Among the tranquility and sophistication, there was also the same sense of hustle as by the Pantheon, with vendors and performers and beggars.

Jacoby studied each fountain, admiring the detail and wishing he could jump into the shallow waters and breaststroke slowly around the gods. He couched his childish impulses and wandered off in search of one of Bill's requirements: paintings by Caravaggio in the church of San Luigi dei Francesi. The small church was nearby and easy to find thanks to helpful signage. The muted light within offered a nice reprieve from the mid-morning glare. Jacoby, as had become his habit, sat in the last row of pews and breathed the sacred air. He was not becoming religious so much as he was connecting with the spirituality offered within the churches themselves. He, of course, marveled at the architecture and opulence, even if the latter struck him as somewhat over the top, but he most appreciated the serenity. Churches in Italy felt so safe, as if he could appreciate the solace they provided over the centuries. It was a similar sentiment he enjoyed in museums, surrounded by the blessings of humanity in all its glory. It affirmed his faith, so often challenged, in mankind and of what they were capable.

The trio of Caravaggio paintings in their private chapel did not disappoint. They all featured a sequence involving St. Matthew, whoever he was, and Jacoby really only cared about the details of each and the way light, somehow on canvas, seemed so real. He stared for a long time at the face of a young boy, in a feather-strewn hat, his face illuminated by a shaft of light. The innocence mixed with trepidation reminded Jacoby of when he was a little boy, when his life was so often interrupted by his father's moves from college teaching post to college teaching post. Jacoby recognized the uncertainty in the boy's face. He had a hard time turning away.

Outside the church, in the actual and fantastic light of Rome, Jacoby skirted the top side of Piazza Navona and, among the buzzing of motorino and mid-morning traffic, followed signs for Castel Sant'Angelo. He could feel and smell the river Tiber before arrival. He walked along the river's precipice, high above the murky, green waters among curved banks with swirling eddies. The land on the other side of the river was low except for St. Peter's Basilica, it's massive cupola dominating the skyline. Jacoby liked how, at least in Rome and Florence, the cities were separated into distinct sections by the river with the smaller "other side" having a more mellow vibe.

The pedestrian, cobble-stoned bridge across the Tiber to Castel Sant'Angelo was adorned on the parapets, appropriately enough, with statues of angels. The short span fed directly to a towering cylinder fortress of brick. Jacoby walked the circumference, noting the scarred brick and ancient wear of a structure that has clearly been through much strife. It felt to Jacoby like a relic from the other side of the Tiber, not quite as antiquated as the colosseum and the forum but still with that motif of ruin. It also felt militant, devoid of soul, and Jacoby was happy that Bill advised him not to enter and to move on toward Vatican City.

St. Peter's Basilica was an easy landmark to pursue and a short distance from Castel Sant'Angelo. The streets were narrow and residential though steady with tourists or pilgrims moving toward and away from Vatican City. The idea that the Catholic church has its own city, and other properties and a major presence around the city, was curious to Jacoby. Rome, in many ways because of this, felt in places like a company town, with the company being not the religion itself but the operations of Catholicism. In his eavesdropping efforts, the Pope's name, "Papa," came up often in conversations both casual and serious, like a local sports hero. Jacoby liked passing the many priests and nuns; they seemed peaceful and kind, dedicated to their life's work, but the omnipresent security apparatus, the serious men in serious suits and sunglasses, wearing earpieces with weapons at their waist, talking into their lapels, moving through the city as if on a mission, bothered Jacoby, as if it belied the essence that made Rome "eternal." The need for such security was also troubling because he recognized the source of such precaution: that left to the ways of man, sans the heavy security apparatus, the Pope and the church in Rome would be gone in a New York minute.

This is why Jacoby admired all religions from afar, appreciating the tribute and accomplishments while ignoring the hypocrisy and ugly truths. It was easy to admire St. Peter's Square, the circular and massive piazza hosting a rocking party of statues with enough room for a few thousand more. The obelisk in the center, quickly becoming one of his favorite signatures of the city (after the fountains, of which the piazza had two), was particularly impressive and appropriate for such a grand setting. It appeared, to Jacoby, to be marking the spot of a very important place. Here! Here! Here!

He walked the courtyard, busy with statues, that accessed the Basilica, stopping before entering to read some information about its construction and artistic contributions over the centuries by an all-star lineup of Italian architects and artists. Most impressive and also mind boggling was the date of the original construction in the 4th century. Jacoby did the math and shook his head, thinking of buildings in Boston from the 1600s that are considered "historic." Humbled and curious, he entered the Basilica and immediately felt like he was on an episode of "Lifestyles of the Rich and Religious."

It wasn't just the scope but the glitz. The interior dazzled with gold and bronze. Even the natural light slotting through stained glass or small windows had a gilded glow. Jacoby thought the massive bronze canopy over the altar would work nicely in a loft, over the bed; then he thought he better get moving before God read his thoughts and zapped him with a lightning bolt, the same feeling he had in churches when cynicism rose after studying the umpteenth painting featuring baby Jesus. Jacoby dashed his minor thoughts of sacrilege by climbing the narrow stairwell up to the top of the cupola. The view was lovely and expansive, but he felt, physically and spiritually, removed from Rome itself. He desired to get back to town.

Chapter 17

The walk away from Vatican City felt like a reprieve, as if he had been visiting somewhere as opposed to experiencing it. He was happy to be experiencing Rome again, meandering quiet streets outside Vatican City with awareness of the river to his left, evident from the slight breeze that carried minerals. He caught what would pass for a main road in the sleepy quarter and followed it toward increased activity. His only landmark was John Cabot University, the American college in Rome where Bill had been immersed in myriad ways during his time living there. Jacoby pondered that romantic existence, of being in a quaint college town environment within a European capital. No wonder Bill was so nostalgic about his years in Rome.

Beyond the college, the neighborhood of Trastevere came to life. The lanes were tighter, slightly more rugged with an increased population density and motorini needling through. The walls, of the same pastel panorama as the rest of the city, crumbled in places and were marked with graffiti. Still, it wasn't the East Village before gentrification or even after. It simply felt like a reprieve from the more austere environment of Rome's center across the river. Just a touch more edge. Still, somewhere nearby, a cello moaned a lovely sonata that drifted through the narrow streets. Jacoby, once again, thought of Oltrarno in Florence and how he missed Helen.

Young people dominated Trastevere, and as Jacoby passed through in the lunch hour, students abound, set free to release their energies, gathering in small corners or in piazzas to frolic and smoke and talk over each other. Jacoby checked his phone for the particular instruction provided by Bill of finding an English-language bookstore called "Almost Corner" where he was to introduce himself to the owner, say hello from Bill, and ask the whereabouts of a particular place to take his lunch. Jacoby was happy to engage in Bill's whimsy and thought of this as a humble way to let those who might be interested know that he was back in town.

Jacoby was hungry, so he cheated and, in English, asked an American girl smoking Italian cigarettes the whereabouts of the bookstore. She rolled her eyes and pointed down the block, "Sempre dritto," she said and turned her head in profile, propping up the elbow of the smoking hand with the fist of the other.

Jacoby thanked her in exaggerated, clumsy-tourist Italian and walked away, happy to be beyond the emotional trappings of youth, though he, once again, envied those studying abroad, even though his situation was much, much better: He would not be returning to America at the end of the semester.

His destination, as advertised, was almost on a corner with the most basic of signage. A small vestibule opened under a gorgeous archway into a cool, fair-sized room of good light, wooden shelves and slate floors, with the smell of paper and ink and just a hint of dust. And lots and lots of books. On the ground level, within the book-lined, floor-to-nearly-ceiling shelves, were tables on the chess-pattern floor stacked with literary offerings. A balcony level above held more books where the only patrons at the moment studied the racked titles. Near the entrance, a middle-aged man in a rumpled polo shirt, wearing circular eyeglasses with the temples tucked into the fair and only hair on his head, was behind the counter staring into a computer screen. Jacoby approached and cleared his throat.

"Hello there," the man said with a kind smile and an Irish accent. "How might I help you?"

"Hi," Jacoby said, readying his voice after hours of inactivity. "Are you Dermot?"

The man tilted his head and some red appeared in his pallor. "I am," he said enthusiastically.

Jacoby stuck out his hand. "I'm Jacoby Pines, from America. Bill Guion asked me to stop by and say hello."

Dermot took Jacoby's hand ever so slightly as his mouth opened. "You can't be serious?"

"I am," Jacoby said, taking his moistened hand back and rubbing it on his pant leg.

"How wonderful," Dermot said looking out the plate glass window to the street before turning his attention back to Jacoby. "Is he here? How is he? Where is he?"

Someone walked in, but Dermot kept his eager eyes on Jacoby, who couldn't help smile at the enthusiasm inspired by the possible return of a long, lost friend. "He's fine," Jacoby answered, "but he's not here. I mean, he is here in Rome, but not here with me now."

"I can see that," Dermot said, somewhat snarky. He snatched off his glasses and cleaned them on his shirt.

Jacoby spoke slowly to project calm and ease the poor man's heart. "We are down from Florence on business, which Bill is taking care of while I walk around Rome following his itinerary."

"I see," Dermot said with an intentionally patient nod. "That would be Bill."

"And he asked me to come by here to say hello and also ask you to point out a restaurant he has in mind for my lunch."

Dermot clasped his hands together and dunked his head forward and back up as he laughed out loud. "Now that is so Bill!" he said, putting a hand on his hip. "I'm glad he hasn't changed."

"I'm pretty sure he hasn't," Jacoby confirmed.

"Well, good," Dermot said. "I will tell you where your lunch is to be had, but you must, in return, tell Bill that his and your presence are required tonight at Popi Popi."

"Popi Popi?" Jacoby repeated with a squint and a smile.

"Yes," Dermot said definitively. "If Bill hasn't changed, as you say, he will get the joke and be there nonetheless. Let's say 8:00?"

"OK," Jacoby agreed. "Now about my lunch..."

Chapter 18

Dermot walked Jacoby out front of the shop and gave him careful directions to the nearby destination. Jacoby, in a narrow lane among the lingering smell of flowers fading from blossom, felt invigorated by the immersion among locals, primarily, as opposed to clusters of tourists. Mostly, though, there was a sense of something momentous coming, but he wasn't sure what it was. He figured that simply having plans for the evening, and a reunion among friends for Bill, most importantly, raised his spirits, lifting him with that precious sense of simple well-being that defined his Italian adventure.

And, of course, there was lunch. The eatery - distinct from the traditional Italian hierarchy of osteria, trattoria, ristorante - had a cheeky, French name, which made Jacoby skeptical upon entry, even knowing that he was in the best of hands with a recommendation from Bill. Through a tiny oasis of potted ferns and ficus trees, on a charming corner with alfresco tables for two on either side of the entrance, booths lined each side of the narrow, interior floor space; the walls stacked high with bottles of wine as the only decor reminded Jacoby of the bookstore's motif dedicated to vino within a luncheonette setting. A ceiling fan turned under the antique ceiling. The chatter was all in Italian, and the aroma had Jacoby's nose twitching and his head spinning with variety. A brusk man approached, his hair and dress shirt disheveled, and snatched a menu from aside the register on the front counter.

"Uno per pranzo," Jacoby said, trying his best to casually request the casual request.

"OK," the man said with a Gallic display of annoyance, as he looked around at the crowded room. There were a few open booths in back, but Jacoby understood the reluctance to give a table for four to a party of one, especially with the lunch hour still in full swing.

"Fuori?" Jacoby suggested over the man's shoulder.

He turned and nodded, a smile tugging at the corners of his mouth. "Bravo," he said quickly and led Jacoby outside.

Jacoby smiled without hesitation at the simple but seamless conversation. They went out front, and Jacoby tucked into a small table covered by the shade of ficus leaves. The street was clean and quiet with no vehicular traffic, the opposite wall of faded ochre with a green door below a window bursting with tangles of ivy. The menu featured a variety of meats and vegetables and pastas, both traditional and somewhat international in origin. Cool. Jacoby knew his order, thanks to Bill, and gave it in Italian to a harried, young waiter, who left the menu per Jacoby's request, and hurried back inside for a bottle of frizzante water and a half carafe of Frascate. Jacoby was thirsty and hungry, having been out walking non-stop for hours, including the 500-some-odd steps to the top of St. Peter's Basilica.

Sipping both water and wine, Jacoby read the menu, recognizing influences from France, Egypt, and Spain among the now familiar offerings of cucina Romana. It was nice to rest and breathe and think freely about pleasant things in the shade in front of a Roman wine bar of international influence. It was nice to thread, ever so slightly, into the context of language and culture and milieu. Jacoby's mastery of Italian menus felt thorough, and he checked off every plate from antipasti to dolci, noting one he desired while the one he had ordered arrived.

The magical experience with a plate of oven roasted chickpeas was among Bill's favorite stories from Jacoby's early days in the hills south of Florence. He had pursued them through curiosity, following his nose, procured them at the local bakery, embraced by everyone there, and finally enjoyed them immensely with fresh focaccia and local wine outside of the village cafe under the auspices of Nicoletta. To Bill, this story was the essence of cucina tipica, and Jacoby recognized the moment as his first embrace of what that moniker truly meant. And he had learned a new word: ceci.

Jacoby's ceci dish in Rome arrived at the table in a small glass bowl with a thick stem. It only resembled Jacoby's previous Italian experience with chickpeas in its faded caramel color, not the circular legume but as a pâté adorned with a sprig of parsley and stuck with a triangle of crisped pita bread. The waiter also left a bottle of olive oil and a ramekin of salt. Jacoby readied his palate with a sip of wine and then spread some of the ceci pâté on the pita. Upon completion of a single bite, his hand shot into the air to get the waiter's attention who was at the register just inside the doorway. He came outside with a concerned look, and Jacoby spoke quickly to assuage his concerns and order a different wine to meet the depth of the dish and also ask for more bread.

"Per favore," he began. "Questo è incredibile, ma ho bisogno un differente vino."

The waiter nodded, as if possibly impressed. Having already culled the wine list, Jacoby knew exactly what he wanted. "Un bicchiere di Vino Nobile di Montepulciano."

The waiter nodded again, definitely impressed. "E un po più pane," Jacoby added a request for a little more bread.

Pleased with himself and ready to eat, Jacoby savored the depth of ceci pâté, clearly supplemented by potato and aromatics, drizzled in peppery olive oil and sprinkled with coarse salt. The wine arrived right away, in a giant goblet, and it took a mighty yet sophisticated red such as it to stand up to earthy decadence of the vegetarian offering.

When finished, Jacoby, satisfied but not sated and still curious about the menu, took a plate of braised oxtail laced with Moroccan spices, and another glass of Vino Nobile. As he ate the succulent meat and wiped up the piquant sauce, he recognized the need for a nap after lunch, especially if they had a big night planned with Bill's old friends.

Chapter 19

Jacoby wandered through Trastevere confident in his sense of direction. He moved away from the course he'd come, but kept the river to the same side for orientation purposes. The streets radiated a distinct energy, one of charm with a thread of transgression. Jacoby now thought of New York's West Village, a tony, safe-haven for gay men; and the East Village where outcasts and rebels dominated. The street Jacoby followed curved toward the river, and when passing more facilities of the American university, under a canopy of sycamore trees above the Tiber's banks, he realized that lunch was the last item on Bill's itinerary, so he called his friend for some direction.

"Ready for a rest?" Bill asked, skipping his normal, mezzo-baritone phone greeting of "Pronto?"

Jacoby laughed. "Should I meet you at our place or in the Campo?"

"Will you be able to find your way home?" Bill asked. "Where are you now?"

Bill's voice sounded buoyant, which pleased Jacoby very much. He was eager to return the feeling and make Bill proud of his fledgling familiarity with Rome.

"I'm crossing Ponte Garibaldi now," Jacoby said, on the bridge near a bend in the Tiber where a tiny island split the current. "What is that?"

"The island to your right, I presume you mean?"

"Yeah," Jacoby confirmed.

"Tiber Island," Bill said. "Home to a hospital and very little else."

"Cool," Jacoby uttered for no good reason other than the fact that there was a tiny island with a large hospital in the middle of Rome's river.

"I guess," Bill halfheartedly concurred, "but if you want something actually cool, cross the street once over the bridge, go left and enjoy a gelato from a shop, oh, half a block down. You can't miss it, and it can't be missed as it is among the best in all of Rome."

"I was just thinking about a gelato," Jacoby said.

"I imagine," Bill purred. "And since you are in the vicinity, after your gelato, which you will take within the shop or out front at a table and not..."

"I know. I know," Jacoby interrupted Bill's familiar tirade about the disgrace of eating anything while walking.

"Good," Bill said. "After you've finished, return back to the road that feeds the bridge, remain on our side. At the first corner, turn to your right and explore the Jewish ghetto."

"OK," Jacoby said. "Am I after anything in particular? A landmark or something? Fried artichokes maybe?"

"Well," Bill said with a soft breath, ignoring the attempt at humor. "You should just walk, slowly, feel the history, but also recognize the cobblestones in front of certain residences."

Jacoby paused, nearly over the bridge. He leaned into the railing and followed the river's path back toward St. Peter's. A breeze lifted his bangs and cooled his forehead. A nun rode by on a bicycle. A siren wailed from an ambulance on its way to the hospital. "What do they represent?" he asked.

"See if you can figure it out on your own," Bill suggested and then changed his tone. "I'll meet you at the bar at 3:00 to discuss and hear all about your day."

"OK," Jacoby agreed, happy to be removed, at least temporarily, from the heavy currency of the conversation about brass cobblestones. "I'll see you then. Ciao."

"Ciao," Bill sang his goodbye but salvaged the conversation before Jacoby could hang up. "Oh! Were you able to find Dermot?"

"Oh, yeah. I did," Jacoby said. "He seems nice."

"He is," Bill said. "Anything else?"

"He wants us to meet him and some others for dinner tonight."

"Where?" Bill asked, skeptically.

"Popi Popi," Jacoby repeated the amusing name.

Bill laughed, and Jacoby could imagine him shaking his lowered head.

"What's so funny?" Jacoby asked, eager to be in on the joke.

"I'll explain later," Bill said. "Enjoy your gelato and your tour. Ciao."

"Ciao," Jacoby said and continued his walk over the bridge, toward his date with a gelato.

·   ·   ·

Under a stretch of shade across the river, Jacoby crossed the busy street and easily found the small gelato shop within a charming storefront. The Gelateria del Teatro, by name, reminded Jacoby of the Teatro del Sale in Florence where Jacoby and Helen, along with Bill, had taken their first meal together on that fantastic evening that had ended in the morning. Only the Italians could make theater out of food.

The street side windows of the gelato shop displayed vibrant fruits, and Jacoby marveled at the range and intensity of colors, just like when walking through the market in the Campo, or walking through any market anywhere in Italy, with the baskets of fruits and vegetables bursting as if they were somehow alive, connected to the earth like flowers and plants still rooted in rich soil. And it really was about the soil, Jacoby often thought, the unique, rich terroir that exists on this peninsula blessed by a loving sun and surrounded by gentle seas. Home field advantage, Jacoby thought. True, but one of which the Italians took full advantage. And Jacoby sought, as he did throughout each day, to validate that advantage as he entered the theater of a gelato shop.

The display, in stainless steel containers stuck with serving spoons, featured a rainbow of smoothed and swirled colors and shades, a candy-store window for all ages. Often a secondary recognition to Jacoby, but rarely lost upon him, was the pristine interiors of Italian vendors of "prodotti" or products. From the offering of raw meats to glistening gelatos, the spaces were immaculate, carefully decorated, aromatic, and exciting. Jacoby often entered shops without hunger or need, simply to be there and enjoy the ambiance. It was similar to his visits to churches, though he was much more devout in his dedication to gastronomy. Typically a taker of a medium gelato cup, offering two flavors, Jacoby - after an unusually large lunch - chose to pair his imperative flavor of pistacchio with strawberry instead of stracciatella, opting for fruit over cream, and also for the opportunity to say "fragola" to the kind woman behind the counter in a clean apron with a cute little cap on her head.

Jacoby took his gelato in the shade out front, at a small table, as traffic zipped past in the dappled sunlight on the street. The strawberry flavor was bright and refreshing, complimenting the pistacchio but also cutting it a bit too much for Jacoby's palate. He'd go back to the vanilla with chocolate chip pleasure of stracciatella next time, and probably every other time after that for the foreseeable future. That important matter resolved, Jacoby discarded his cup and returned up the road to the mouth of the bridge where he would follow Bill's instructions to find and experience the Jewish ghetto.

He arrived within minutes and immediately felt a slight shift in vibe. In contrast to Trastevere's distinction from the rest of the city, the Jewish ghetto felt dated, even forlorn. It was no "ghetto" in the American sense, the consistent Roman architecture on display, but the facades were just slightly more faded than in other parts of the city, the wear a little more pronounced. The time when it was actually a ghetto lingered like a ghost not seen but present.

Still, it was a lovely quarter, with many outdoor eateries on the wide lanes, piazzas with fountains and even some ruins. Three kids took turns kicking a soccer ball against a wall. Artisans worked within shops behind curtains that billowed in a breeze summoned by the sun's descent. Jacoby kept to the shade, feeling the effect of autumn sun on his face and forearms after another long day of exposure. And within those shadows, passing the street-side residences, he stumbled upon his first set of worn brass cobblestones. "Here lived..." the engraving began and then provided a name and a date. The impact was immediate on Jacoby: the connection between Jews and Europe and history. He heard marching boots on the cobblestones and screams of people being torn away from their homes. He touched his face, and it was wet with tears. Longing and loss overwhelmed him, that of others and that of his own. "Mommy," he said in his little boy voice, once again under massive duress that summoned his mother for the second time upon arriving in Italy.

Jacoby stumbled off, fleeing the visceral agony the golden stones aroused, as easy as the setting sun had summoned the breeze that flitted through the Jewish ghetto. Upon a fountain, Jacoby took some cool water and rinsed his face of tears. His emotional vulnerability was something he tried to suppress, and he was successful for the most part, but there was no avoiding or overcoming the excruciating fact that he was, for the majority of his life, a motherless child.

Chapter 20

Jacoby drifted out of the Jewish ghetto and found a train line to follow until he reached the square at Torre Argentina. He leaned into the rail and looked over the ruined temples and theater. Cats mewed among the sacred grounds. Umbrella pines framed the distance under a blanket of blue sky. Jacoby blinked and breathed until his head began to clear. The reckoning with reality was something he had to do from time to time, to remember that life was not a fantasy, to stay in touch with the hard truth that being alive was no easy task, to varying degrees, to all creatures on the planet. He had a hurt that would never go away. He had suffered through epic bouts of loneliness as a child and adolescent, depression and disappointment as an adult. Still, for the most part, he'd been quite lucky so far in life. He felt somewhat ashamed and certainly humbled to be so fortunate as he was, to grow up privileged in America and adore the life he now had in Italy.

Walking back to Campo de' Fiori, along Corso Vittorio Emanuele II, the slanted sunlight of late afternoon in his eyes, Jacoby vowed to remain diligent in his humility, to stay aware of his blessings, to keep them always in mind, and to project his grace upon others. And the other he kept thinking of, more so than ever since arriving in Rome, was Bill. The memory of Filippo must be with him always, and especially excruciating in Rome, where their love was born and where it blossomed. Jacoby hoped that the dinner with old friends would serve as a balm, but he wasn't sure. He'd do his best to keep an eye on Bill and stay close all night.

A text message jarred the phone in Jacoby's pocket. Hoping it was Helen reaching out at such an appropriate time, he pulled it out quickly to study the screen.

"Cheers, x cousin in law!" the message from Dolores read. "I plan 2 attend the soirée at the consortium. And to inspect the villa. No need to pick me up. I've arranged a new car for the occasion!"

Jacoby laughed and shook his head. Speaking of privileged, there was no one he had ever met privy to such entitlements as Dolores, yet she was somehow aware of it. She didn't go out of her way to help people, nor did she make any attempt to cover her brutal snobbery. She lived her life conscious of who she was and all she had. Jacoby admired her for that, and he was particularly appreciative of her business acumen, swooping in to pick up the villa and a share of the consortium both at bargain prices. In the process, she had saved many jobs and helped many lives, including his own as he would manage the property one day and live on the grounds once owned by his family.

He tapped a quick note back to Dolores, and made note to himself of yet another blessing in the form of his outrageous former cousin-in-law to be. Passing the church of Sant'Andrea, watching parishioners enter on their way home from work, Jacoby recognized why the devout mark their days with such an act, a daily reminder that they are lucky to be alive. Jacoby thought about entering the church for a quick moment of reflection, but he was more intrigued by recognizing his blessings in the form of an aperitivo with his friend.

•   •   •

Bill was resting at their usual outside table when Jacoby arrived at the bar. The waitress smiled knowingly at him and looked lovingly at the dozing Bill. Jacoby returned her smile and signaled their order with two fingers. She nodded and went inside.

"Oh, hello Jacoby," Bill said immediately after opening his eyes. "How was your gelato?"

Jacoby sat down in the shade and felt his weary body relax into the wood and wicker chair. "The gelato was great," he said, "but the brass cobblestones were a little too much to bear."

"I understand," Bill said, threading his fingers in front of his chest, his elbows propped on the chair's arms. He stared at the end of his nose and did not speak.

Their drinks arrived and Bill thanked the waitress kindly, raised his glass to Jacoby and cleared his throat before speaking. "To loss," he said with mock-seriousness. "The worst damn thing in the whole damn world."

Jacoby smirked and raised his glass. Bill nodded. They drank their spritzes in silence, watching the market breakdown and shadows arrive over the Campo de' Fiori. It was still early, and they had hours before dinner. Jacoby ordered two more drinks, and Bill signaled his approval, sitting up some, his content squint in place.

"Looking forward to seeing your old friends?" Jacoby asked.

"Most of them," Bill remarked.

"Not all?"

"It's an expat crowd of gay men," Bill said. "A couple of the hens can be tiresome."

Jacoby liked when Bill got snarky. It seemed to open a valve and release some internal pressure. "Well," Jacoby said. "I'll look forward to meeting them. Hens and all."

Insouciance informed Bill's eyes, and Jacoby knew his friend was in a good mood and looking forward to their night out in Rome. When the drinks were watery, Jacoby flagged the waitress.

"Posso pagare?" he asked if he could pay.

"Certo," she responded and went off for the check.

Bill stood up and placed a large key on the table in front of Jacoby. "I assume you've done enough walking for one day," he said. "I certainly have not."

"Where are you going?" Jacoby asked.

"Just for a quick walk to check in on Caravaggio."

"Tell him I was impressed."

"I shall," Bill said, nodded and then walked off into the piazza.

Jacoby paid the check and made some chit chat with the waitress. He was tired, emotionally and physically, and looking forward to a nap. After strolling the piazza, practicing his Italian gait, studying the shops and nodding at vendors, he said "Ciao" to Mamma making pasta in the storefront; she smiled and said "Ciao" in return.

At the door to their residence, key in hand, Jacoby paused. Something beckoned him into the courtyard next door. He entered the open area cloaked in muted shadow and diffuse light. It was cool and silent except for the gurgling fountain. He took a few steps in and looked around. There was no one there, but he didn't feel alone.

Chapter 21

Darkness sifted down on Rome as Jacoby and Bill walked the lamp-lit lanes from Campo de' Fiori towards Trastevere. Rested and refreshed, the two friends did not speak, their silence matching the still of the night. Jacoby appreciated the calm of Italian evenings, the hush that soothed at the end of the day. The streets where they walked, reserved for foot traffic only, were mostly empty in the in-between hours after work and before most Italians set out for dinner. The non-native Italians were on expat hours, navigating their adopted city at their own schedule.

They stopped on Ponte Sisto so Jacoby could take a picture of the river streaked with moonlight, with the light-ringed cupola of St. Peter's Basilica in the distance. He texted it to Helen accompanied by the cliché, "Wish you were here."

She texted back before he could even return the phone to his pocket. "Cheesy! But I do have some time soon. When are you coming home? Or should I come there????"

"Lemme check," he wrote back. "XO."

There was a long-haired, shirtless guitarist sitting on the bridge with his back to the railing doing a decent job with "Stairway to Heaven" and a lot of young people on the bridge and in the small square on the Trastevere side. Bill was waiting patiently at the end of the bridge, the young revelers to his back, with his hands latched behind him. Jacoby sidled up and plopped a wrist over Bill's shoulder as they turned in sync to walk toward their destination.

"So, how are we making out down here?" he asked.

"You're curious about our progress," Bill responded.

"Yeah," Jacoby said. "Are we progressing Italian style?"

"Actually, there has been progress," Bill confirmed. "And I suspect we will be free to return to Florence early next week."

"Next week?" Jacoby asked, amused. "What day is today?"

Bill laughed. "Always the sign of time well spent," he mused. "Today is Friday."

Jacoby shook his head and acknowledged the energized and temporarily liberated throng of young people gathered in the open area as he and Bill passed into the mouth of a narrow lane lined with eateries. The aroma of fledgling kitchens, of sauces simmering, meats roasting and vegetables sautéing sparked Jacoby's hunger.

"What's the speciality at Popi Popi," he asked.

"Pizza," Bill answered.

"Cool," Jacoby said. "I could go for a pizza."

"No you won't," Bill said.

"What?"

"You won't be having pizza at Popi Popi or anywhere else in Rome," Bill said casually as he peered into the restaurants they passed.

Jacoby stopped in his tracks at the comment and then hurried to catch up to Bill. "What do you mean?" he asked, laughing. "Isn't Rome, like, known for pizza?"

Bill turned and took Jacoby's shoulders in his hands. "My dear boy," he began. "The only cardinal sin while in Rome, for gastronomes at least, is pizza. And you are absolutely forbidden from ordering any."

"Forbidden?" Jacoby chuckled, though thrown somewhat by Bill's serious look and the fingers digging into his shoulders.

"Forbidden," Bill confirmed, tapping Jacoby twice on the cheek, like a mob boss, before relaxing both hands down and resuming their walk. "Tomorrow being Saturday, I will take you to Naples for real pizza. Tonight at Popi Popi, I will order the food and you pick the wines. D'accordo?"

"D'accordo," Jacoby agreed and wondered what the night had in store for them.

· · ·

The group of eight men, all white and decidedly non-Italian in complexion and fashion sense, were seated at a long table in the front of the restaurant, just inside the panels opened to the street. White curtains billowed around the empty chairs at the end. The group could have easily been some middle-aged-to-older men on holiday together, dressed like tourists and speaking English in various accents. They stood in unison upon Bill's arrival and took turns greeting him with hugs, compliments and kisses on each cheek. After an individual turn with Bill, each man, with the exception of Dermot who smiled at Jacoby like an old friend, introduced himself with handshakes ranging from firm to fey.

They seemed, to Jacoby, like a perfectly decent group of men, and their adoration of Bill was obvious and endearing. Clearly, Bill had not been in touch as the questions came non-stop, informed by urgency and hints of pique at the excommunication. Bill, sitting at the head of the table by the open panels, with his legs crossed and his chin up, patiently answered all of the questions and ignored or swatted away the barbs. If he had felt badly about not being in touch, it did not show in his answers nor demeanor. When the queries slowed, a sense of rhythm and ambiance ensued, a mood more typical of a regular dinner among friends. And then suddenly, one of the men, the youngest of them and the most effeminate with some eyeliner, bleached blonde hair, red capri pants and white t-shirt, both too tight, asked Jacoby, for the whole table to hear, if he and Bill were lovers.

Jacoby was taken aback both from his role as an observer and by the question itself. The inquiry had been made before, through crude commentary by the hunters back in the village, but he assumed such talk belonged only to macho assholes who wondered about such things. The other men were slightly embarrassed, hands on chests and askance looks at the questioner, but they soon turned their eyes to Bill for an answer.

"Jacoby and I are friends, and very good ones at that," Bill answered politely and with pride. "We are also business partners in a new hotel in the village of Antella in Firenze Sud, a property once owned by Filippo's family, and acquired in most dramatic fashion. Once we get some of the legal matters settled here in Rome, you are each invited to visit anytime, though not all together. Good god."

The men inquired about the story Bill had mentioned, especially the professorial types together at the far end who Jacoby assumed worked at the university. One of them, a large, well-mannered, wholesome-looking American in a beige, linen blazer over a white dress shirt, insisted Bill tell the entire story.

Bill agreed to gladly do so after ordering. Every single one of the other men asked for pizza, each shooting Bill a sideways glance or a snarky face after doing so. Bill sat dignified with an amused smirk flattening his lips.

"Very well," he said when all orders, except for his and Jacoby's, had been placed. The waiter stood between them, and Bill motioned with his hand for a moment of patience before addressing the table. "Would you all be kind enough, in light of your horrendous palates and my appreciation of seeing you all again, allow us to choose and pay for your wine?"

"By all means," the kindly professor said on behalf of the table. "Thank you."

"Go right ahead," Dermot chimed, eyes widening behind his thick frames.

Bill nodded. "Jacoby," he posed, "would you do the honor."

Jacoby picked up the wine list and culled the section of reds. Keeping in mind the orders of mostly Pizza Margherita and a few with mushrooms or truffles, he identified the ideal pairing a minute after perusing began. He cleared his throat and addressed the waiter. "Due bottiglie della Vecchia Terre Di Montefili Chianti Classico Riserva," he said properly without pause or stumble, feeling the words form in his mouth and escape his tongue. He realized in that moment that it not only sounded good but it also actually felt good to speak Italian well. The waiter nodded, as if impressed, and walked away.

"Bravo," Bill said to Jacoby and then ordered for them a fritto misto of fish and vegetables, a plate of pasta with clams and then a whole roasted branzino. He also asked for a bottle of Pecorino wine from the Le Marche region before explaining to Jacoby that the wine had nothing to do with the cheese of the same name and the bottle he ordered, from a producer named Cocci Grifoni, was among the best in the country.

Jacoby was trained in advance, by this point, to agree with Bill's assessments, and he was eager to taste a new wine. He was also ready for some seafood since there wasn't much fish on menus in Florence, and it was even harder to find out in the countryside with the Tuscan coast being nearly 100 kilometers away, well beyond the Italian ethos of locally sourced eating usually not extending beyond the area within eyesight.

Bill told a somewhat abridged story of how he and Jacoby had met, what they had in common and how they unsuccessfully pursued Filippo's mother in hopes of evoking her mercy and acceptance by showing her the photograph of her disappeared daughter that Jacoby had brought from America. He included the part about Jacoby slaying the cinghiale and saving the sagra, as well, and, of course, the miraculous ending involving the settlement of Jacoby's wrongful termination suit back in the States on the very day the hotel went up for auction and the two of them had become business partners.

"How fantastic," the professor declared. "That needs to be in a book."

Bill laughed. "I can't imagine readers being interested in an old fag and a young American running around like imbeciles trying, unsuccessfully I might add, to find a dying matriarch," he said.

"Not quite *The DaVinci Code*," Dermot noted.

"You'd be surprised," the professor continued. "People love reading anything about Italy. Look at *Under the Tuscan Sun*, nothing really happens in that book at all, besides the renovation of a villa, and everyone under the sun, it seems, read that."

The men nodded in acknowledgment, and the one in red capri pants said, "Loved that movie," much to the embarrassment of his friends who shook their heads and tisked.

"And how about *Eat Pray Love*," another man added. "Poor girl had orgasms just from eating gelato, and everyone fell over themselves about that."

There was laughter around the table, and Bill put the conversation to rest by promising, disingenuously, to keep the book project in mind, just as the food arrived.

Jacoby couldn't detect any problems with the pizza from the aroma, and he was envious of the flavors the men enjoyed, along with the distinct, visceral experience from physically eating pizza. He missed it. Of course, the fish courses, from the nearby coast, did not disappoint. The fritto misto platter filled Jacoby's mouth with the song of sardines and squid, sweet potatoes and zucchini, lightly fried and seasoned; the tiny clams had a distinct brininess that worked perfectly with the fresh linguini clung with herbs and oil and a dusting of bread crumbs; and the whole branzino, a visual masterpiece, separated from the skeleton into flaky, flavorful chunks of tender flesh.

The men devoured the bottles of Chianti Classico Riserva, taking a third, along with their pizzas. They asked the waiter to remember the wine for subsequent visits before requesting separate checks, while Bill and Jacoby were still into their second plate, in order to make an event that evening at a nearby bar. Bill waived off their apologies about leaving prematurely, and he assured them that he and Jacoby would join later. Then Bill ordered a second bottle of the Pecorino for him and Jacoby to enjoy with the rest of their meal.

Chapter 22

The sky above the roofline was a blacktop splattered with stars. The street scene echoed with chatter and shimmered in the light thrown from wrought iron lamps on posts or above doorways. Eateries and enotecas quivered with capacity. Sexual tension abounded. Jacoby followed Bill on their after-dinner excursion through the energized section of Trastevere teeming with couples and groups, dressed stylishly in general and even to the point, in some cases, of absurdity. Jacoby was often dumbfounded imagining the decision to buy heels of a certain height or pants of a particular pattern or color or material, to wear a shirt unbuttoned to the naval or a top with a neckline that plunged way past cleavage. He admired the hats on the middle-aged men and the perfume of the women. Italians, even in the fashion extreme, of all ages, were so beautiful and fun to observe, and Jacoby was happy to be out in these hours, in this environment, to get a different look at them.

The ambiance changed as Bill led them away from the crowded piazzas and corners, down abandoned alleys only alive with sparse lights and nocturnal creatures. After a missed turn and then another, concern came over Jacoby since silence and shadows in the city, especially when lost, could be menacing. He worried about Bill's recollection of these hidden corners of Rome after so many years away. A cat fight broke out behind a crumbling wall, and Jacoby's neck tingled.

"Want me to use Google Maps?" he asked. "To find the place."

"No. No," Bill said quickly as they turned a corner to an alley with a dull light shining on figures out front smoking. "And here we are."

The voices of the smokers became audible as they approached, and Jacoby was glad that the young women spoke English. There was no other sound.

"Where are we, anyway?" Jacoby asked as they arrived at a small storefront without signage. Through the smudged, paned windows a woman with shorn yellow hair sang an elegiac song and played acoustic guitar under a single light in a corner by the bar.

"This, my dear boy, is Garbo Bar," Bill said. "Rome's best kept secret, especially for its expat open microphone on Friday nights, though the room is so small there is no need for an actual microphone."

They slipped past the smokers into the cramped room. The low ceiling was lined with wooden beams and the walls were of stones plastered together. It smelled of musk and spilled drinks, centuries of no sunlight. The tables, a loosely arranged assortment of refurbished and incongruous antiques, were filled to the limited capacity. Bill's group of expat friends, occupying a far section of the room that fronted the bar, waved them over, pointing at saved seats on a cushioned bench against the wall. Bill returned the wave and led Jacoby by the arm past the singer and the crowded tables.

The bartender, a burly, jovial young man with unruly black hair and a waxed mustache, in a shirt patterned with hula dancers, wiggled his fingers at Bill and offered a zany smile. Bill veered toward him, but the young man gestured with a flicked wrist to go-on, go-on towards the vacant seats. Bill nodded and continued on as the song ended and applause ensued. Bill and Jacoby said their hellos to the reunited dinner companions and sat on the bench. The room was stuffy with body heat, and Jacoby was reminded of the minuscule, Irish cafe his band used to love to play on St. Mark's Place in the East Village.

"This used to be a stable," Bill leaned toward Jacoby and said, "Where an aristocratic family would keep their horses."

"Smells like it," Jacoby said with his head tilted in Bill's direction.

Bill laughed as the bartender approached with a Negroni in each hand. He handed them both to Jacoby and opened his arms to Bill, who stood for a warm hug. Bill introduced Jacoby to the bartender, and they shook hands. "These are on me," he said about the drinks. "Your drinks the rest of the evening will be on the house, though you'll have to come get them yourselves as table service is a one time thing, babies."

"Why, thank you," Bill said.

Jacoby thanked him, as well, and the bartender returned to his post as the next guest was being introduced by a strawberry blonde who wore her hair in a pompadour and had been sitting with the previous performer at a table in front of the makeshift stage. Through a thick Scottish accent, she welcomed an American writer who was in Rome as a visiting professor at the university. He was close to Jacoby's age, slightly older, well-groomed, slack yet hip in a New York way, short black hair, black t-shirt tucked into black jeans, red Puma Clydes, a yellow pack of cigarettes poking from a pocket of his pants. Much of the front of the room appeared to be students or younger faculty who applauded and whooped with great enthusiasm after the introduction. The author expressed earnest appreciation in a charming, gruff manner, and then read a short story, just written, about the ghost of a childhood friend from Queens who he encountered in a hidden courtyard near Campo de' Fiori.

It was a touching story, beautifully detailed, full of pathos, and threaded with humor. Jacoby had a hard time keeping his shoulders from shaking, remembering the odd feeling he had in that courtyard the night before. The author, at the story's end, pausing and smirking to remain composed, took a breath and said his thanks before joining some companions at a table near the door who stood to greet him with hugs and handshakes. Many of the students came over to offer praise or caught his attention from where they sat. The applause lasted many minutes, and the hostess held up her hands to calm the room and keep the night moving.

"That was splendid," she said. "Hate to have to follow that, but somebody has to if the night is to continue. Can we have a volunteer?"

"This is where things get interesting," Bill leaned toward Jacoby to say.

"How's that?"

"Well, if there isn't a volunteer from the crowd, somewhat not already scheduled to perform, they shut the bar down."

"Uh-oh," Jacoby moaned. "We just got here."

"Yes," Bill added, "but if they can get a performer, we will be free to stay all night."

Jacoby thought of his previous all-nighter with Bill, where he and Helen had danced with Brazilian trannies while Bill was off with a rent boy, and he was ambivalent about the prospects of another such night here in Rome.

People were chattering among themselves, avoiding the awkwardness that swept around the room, until Dermot stood up and declared, "I think it would be appropriate for Bill Guion to read upon his return to Rome and Garbo Bar."

The men around them all turned to Bill and offered encouragement. Bill blushed and shook his head with insistence. "You're a writer?" Jacoby asked him.

"Well, yes," Bill said. "I practiced journalism for thirty years professionally and wrote poetry in my spare time, some of which I would share here on occasion, often to keep the bar open all night if there were no other volunteers."

"I would have loved to have seen that," Jacoby said and then went to the bar to replenish their drinks before it possibly closed. The men around them continued to cajole Bill, and while Jacoby was at the bar waiting for the drinks, much of the room, many calling Bill by name, had joined the campaign of persuasion. It was cute: a diverse group of ages and backgrounds and nationalities collectively encouraging a septuagenarian expat from Texas to read poetry to keep a hidden Roman bar open all night. Bill, looking meek and fatigued when Jacoby returned with the drinks, shot to his feet. The room cheered. Bill held up his hands in a request for quiet that quickly came.

"No. No," he said, his voice raised in volume and lowered in pitch. "I have nothing prepared, and I simply am unable to do anything extemporaneously at this point in my life and, particularly, at this point in the evening." He took a Negroni from Jacoby and held it up to the room to indicate that he'd been drinking for quite a while.

There was laughter and quips of disappointment. Bill held a hand back up."But I do know of a way to continue the evening," he offered with an optimistic tone and the glass raised. He shot a quick look at Jacoby, and Jacoby's stomach wrenched inward before Bill continued, "And that would be for my friend and wonderful musician, Jacoby Pines, to play a few songs for us on the guitar."

Initially, Jacoby felt anger toward Bill, almost betrayal, but then he saw the happiness in his friend's face, the much needed socialization and support. Bill's face was alive, much like, Jacoby imagined, when he was young and in love and part of a community in Rome. Jacoby also felt the call of the crowd and remembered the exhilaration of playing music in front of people and why people, like him, picked up a guitar in the first place. The yellow haired woman raised her instrument as an offer, and Jacoby approached, surrounded by applause and curious anticipation, a drink in hand and his head spinning.

The guitar was a solid Yamaha with medium strings. His eyes adjusted to the overhead light as he sat on the stool. He lifted his head and knew it would take a moment to register the collection of faces focused on him. The band Jacoby played in had only one show at a decent-sized music venue, opening for some reunited rockers on their way through Boston, and while the rest of the band lost their shit over the experience, Jacoby thought the gig was a drag. He preferred the intimate places, cafes and bars and venues built for sound and connection to the audience while connecting the audience to each other. His dream would have been to play juke joints around the American south. The former stable in Rome could pass for a European juke joint, and he faced a room of students, academics, and gay men encouraging him with their silent attention and kind expressions.

"Hello," Jacoby said, his voice lowered to adjust to the only key he could remotely pull off. He was no singer, but he knew some tricks to get by.

"Hello," much of the room said back to him, an orchestra of disparate voices and accents.

A short song list came to him in the moment as he recalled some of the songs he'd been toying around with back in the barn, songs he had been playing for years. The warm reception calmed him enough to focus on his breath and let his memory, guided by focus, take him through the physical and mental process of playing an instrument and singing at the same time. The pick was thinner than his preference and slippery in his fingertips, but he found the right grip and dragged it down the strings while fingering an open C chord. Then the quasi-complicated Bm7 chord favored by Bob Dylan. He tuned the A string. He did the same chord change a few times and decided he was ready.

"I came to Italy on vacation four months ago," Jacoby said with a straight face. "And I decided to never leave."

He smiled among the laughter and applause, and Jacoby, empowered by his decision to endear himself to the audience through storytelling, continued. "My friend Bill once told me the only thing he missed about America was breakfast. The only thing I miss about America is Bob Dylan."

He broke into "Po' Boy," a jaunty number from Dylan's *Love & Theft* album. The quick, distinct chord changes, lovely yet discordant, set the backdrop for a narrative of vignettes rooted in the American mythology of suffering, belied, somewhat, by Dylan's playful phrasing. It wasn't close to one of the singer's most popular songs, and Jacoby doubted anyone had heard it before, which is why he mentioned the originator to establish some ethos.

Whatever the reason, the Dylan reference or Jacoby's rendition, or both, the room responded warmly at the song's ending. They clapped vigorously and whooped. Bill, who had been standing the whole time, circled his hands around his mouth and trumpeted "Bravo." Relief swept through Jacoby, followed by a rush of triumph. The room became more vivid, the faces and attire coming into sharper focus. Young people were recording the performance on cell phones. He sipped his drink that had gone watery while he sang, but the melted ice felt good in his dry mouth and throat.

"This one's by another great American musician with a great American name: Muddy Waters," Jacoby said, playing the recognition factor once again. Heads nodded as Jacoby lowered his own to focus on the frets and strings where he would work the sliding opening of "Mean Old Frisco Blues" followed by a succession of hammer-ons and single note runs that preceded the lyrical verses over swinging chord progressions. The song was intricate, especially for the blues, but one of Jacoby's favorites, the single song he had spent the most time mastering. Having done so made him a better guitar player, and having this song in his repertoire made him happy, never more so than killing it at a crowded, hidden bar somewhere in the back alleys of Rome.

The last song was easy to play and sing, and an ode to Italy's obsession with Pearl Jam. Jacoby didn't even set it up, just breaking into the lyrics and chords that began in unison of "Elderly Woman Behind the Counter in a Small Town." The simple progression allowed Jacoby to relax his focus enough to notice the young people sitting up straight and following along, some still filming, and the happy faces on Bill and his crowd. Jacoby could also feel the sweat on his back and a tad of fatigue, from being out of regular practice, creep into his left wrist and fingertips. He was also running out of throat and knew this would be his last song, so he added pathos to the emphasis of certain lyrics and waited for some of those in the know to sing "Hello" with him at the appropriate time. They did, and Jacoby brought the rest of the song home with as much passion and style as he could, swaying back and forth and pretending, if only for a minute, that he was the rock star he once dreamed of being.

When the song was finished, the crowd called for more, but Jacoby knew when to quit, to walk away with them wanting more. He rose from the stool and carefully leaned the guitar against the wall. He exchanged kisses on both cheeks with the guitar's owner and her partner. "Brilliant," the latter said. "You'll have to come back as a scheduled guest."

Jacoby's mouth opened as he imagined coming to Rome for regular gigs. "What a great idea," he said. "I would love that."

"Let's exchange information then," she said with smiling eyes, "before your friends come and get you shitty."

Dermot was closing in, followed by a few others from their group, with a Negroni and a face full of appreciation. The host's name was Finley, and she and Jacoby swapped phone numbers and email addresses. People were up from their seats and mingling, crowding the bar or going outside to smoke. Jacoby accepted the drink from Dermot and was chatting with some of the students when the author from New York approached.

"That was great, man," he said and swung an open hand toward Jacoby from the side. "I really enjoyed it."

"Thanks," Jacoby said, relieved that they had stuck the handshake. "Nice job, as well."

"Cin. Cin," the author said and held up his beer bottle. The two men tapped glass and took sips. The students faded away from the conversation. "I hear you on never wanting to leave. I've been here a month, and I'm already like, fuck New York."

Jacoby made a knowing face and raised his glass again. "I gotta tell you something about your story," he said.

"Really?" the author asked, his dark brows crinkling. "What's that?"

Music came on, a song from the Waterboys, too loud and through creaky speakers. The author looked annoyed by the audio interruption.

"Let me get a smoke," Jacoby suggested. "And I'll tell you outside."

"Bet," the author said and motioned with his head toward the door.

The night cooled Jacoby's still-warm body. Sweat dried quickly on his back and neck. It felt good to be outside, and he breathed the chilled autumn air as they walked a few paces down the alley, out of earshot from the small groups right out front. A harvest moon, jaundiced and oblong, hung low in the velvet sky. Jacoby smelled things, behind a crumbling wall, struggling to grow in the last throes of the season.

"Here you go," the author said, extending his pack of American Spirits.

"Thanks," Jacoby said, pulling out a cigarette by the filter and putting it between his lips.

The author snapped open a Zippo lighter and ignited both ends of their cigarettes. The men took drags and blew smoke toward the moon. The author looked at Jacoby without saying anything. He put a hand in his front pocket and raised his chin.

"OK," Jacoby began. "So that story you read, about your friend."

"Yeah," the author acknowledged.

"That courtyard you mentioned, where you felt, you know, his presence," Jacoby continued.

"Yeah."

"It's right next to the place where I'm staying, literally two steps from our door," Jacoby said.

"Oh, cool," the author said and looked away to take a slow drag.

Jacoby spoke quickly to assuage his listener's disappointment. "I was in there last night, and I could feel someone with me, but there was no one around."

The author's head jerked back to Jacoby. "That's what happened to me," he said and patted his chest. "I'd been here two fucking days, and I don't know how I found that place. I was just wandering around and it, you know, called me in or something. Strangest thing. I was like half-mesmerized and half scared out of my shit."

"Someone's in there," Jacoby said. "I thought it was Bill's lover."

The writer looked around and then back at Jacoby with serious eyes. "Funny you mention him," he said, pulling the skin on his neck.

"Why's that?"

"Now, I've never met this guy, Bill," he said with great care and both hands up. "But some of that crowd you're with, I know them from the university, and we hang out, not all the time, but often enough. It's a small world over here."

"OK," Jacoby followed without following.

"And once in a while they mention him," he said. "This guy Bill."

"Why?" Jacoby interrupted. "What for?"

The author shrugged. "I mean, it's probably nothing, but - his partner's name was Filippo, right?"

"Right," Jacoby confirmed with impatience.

"Well, those guys claim, once in a while, that they see Filippo around Rome," he said. "And not like a ghost but in the flesh."

"Get the fuck out of here," Jacoby insisted and then held up a hand in apology.

"No worries, man," the author said. "It's pretty heavy shit, I know, but I've heard them talking about it on more than one occasion. It's like a game almost, you know? Where's Filippo? Kinda morbid, if you're asking me."

"Are they serious?" Jacoby asked. "I mean, maybe it's just someone who looks like him?"

"I dunno," the author said, "but I just thought to tell you since, you know, it kind of came up all on its own."

"Yeah, thanks," Jacoby said, his head spinning and his heart walloping. He dropped the cigarette and went inside to get Bill out of Garbo Bar.

Chapter 23

The train warbled through the outskirts of Rome, past the industrial fringes blotted by large apartment buildings with balconies used for storage and clothes lines. The southbound, high-speed train would arrive in Naples in just over an hour. Bill and Jacoby were alone in a Business Class car having caught an early departure on a Saturday morning. Their business in Naples involved pizza.

Bill was serene. Dressed comfortably and well-rested, he had thanked Jacoby, once again, for rescuing him from Garbo Bar before things got messy and overextended. Jacoby's agenda was not to save them from a long night but to spare Bill any knowledge of the "Where's Filippo?" game of rumors that might spill from Negroni-stained lips. Jacoby was pissed at Bill's friends for such a cavalier and potentially cruel exercise, and he vowed to find ways to avoid them upon their return to Rome.

That day, though, was for pizza and a quick tour of Naples. Jacoby found it charming that Bill insisted on only eating pizza in Naples, though he also suspected it was more about nostalgia than gastronomy. He and Filippo took regular excursions to Naples for pizza and opera, respective passions they shared with each other. Jacoby was eager for the pizza and curious about Naples, another Italian city of which he only had a murky image. His anticipation heightened as the train picked up speed and the treeline whizzed by the windows.

Bill studied the trees and sky while Jacoby texted with Helen before putting his phone away. He was aware of how hard it could be to be in the company of someone in a relationship, especially when you are alone. The ambient whooshing and gentle rocking of the fast train lulled Jacoby into a cat nap, and he dreamed of being a little boy, eating ice cream with his mother outside a shop in the small town in New Jersey where they had lived. It was the first time he had that dream, and he woke suddenly, sweaty under his tucked chin, wondering if the dream was inspired by memory or imagination.

"Are you all right?" Bill asked.

"Yeah," Jacoby said, wiping his neck. "I've been having the strangest dreams."

"Me as well," Bill shared with nonchalance.

"Maybe we're on to something?" Jacoby suggested with a smile.

Bill laughed. "No," he said. "I imagine not."

"Why not?"

"Oh," Bill began with a hint of melancholy. "I'm past believing that something, anything is coming."

Jacoby leaned toward Bill, cleared his throat, and began an exaggerated, gravely Bob Dylan impersonation. "Last night the wind was whispering something. I was trying to make out what it was," he sang confidentially. "I tell myself something's coming, but it never does."

"Exactly," Bill said with a nod. "Though, there is pizza coming for us and rather soon."

Jacoby smiled at the good news and Bill's enthusiasm, though he was saddened by his friend's rising cynicism. He wondered what had happened to their shared belief in fate as a gift that could not be taken away.

.   .   .

The vast train station in Naples was nearly empty but intense. There seemed to be a grainy shade of gray over everything. The olive faces were furrowed; the people rushed, their Neapolitan dialect obvious and foreign to Jacoby's ears. Outside, fronting a massive piazza, the streets roared with a cacophony of shrill, piercing sounds of sirens and muscular engines, but the pristine Italian sky of kodachrome blue extended over everything and comforted Jacoby with its familiarity. He could also smell the sea. There were mountains in the distance.

They crossed the piazza and walked a wide boulevard lined with stores teeming with Saturday morning activity. The buildings were older and bigger than those in Florence and Rome; the architecture more diverse, less dynamic; the offerings in the stores more prosaic. The air cooled as the sun became a pearl behind a thin stretch of clouds coming in from the coast. A slight scent of sulfur arrived on the breeze.

The port appeared along with a sense of grandeur. There were islands in the distance. They walked near the waterfront past a magnificent castle. Further along, within the vicinity of a grand piazza, was an impressive palace and a powerful theater with a facade of arches and columns that seemed to capture the beautiful masculinity that defined Naples in Jacoby's first impression. It also reminded him of the excursions Bill and Filippo would take for opera and pizza.

"We about ready for that pizza?" Jacoby asked.

"Almost," Bill said, the breeze off the water tangling his gray hair into a nest. "First we need to go see Jesus."

"Jesus?" Jacoby asked. "What's he doing here?"

"Resting," Bill said. "Come on."

They turned away from the water and toward the city center where the streets were narrow. In the cool shadows, among the small storefronts and residences right off the street, a sense of mystery exuded. Jacoby imagined muggings by knife point. Voices were hushed and eyes slanted in suspicion. Jacoby fought the temptation to peer through open doorways and smudged windows with residents mere steps away. He felt so nosy but couldn't turn away, though he did instantly at the hard glares from hard faces. A rogue drop of rain landed on the crown of Jacoby's head, and he felt like he was in a film noir.

Down another alley, they were upon a modest chapel. The silent interior glowed with golden light. Worshipers gathered for a reverential service among candles and murmur. Jacoby followed Bill down marble stairs into a catacomb where they waited behind a few groups in front of something he could not yet see. He sensed Bill's anticipation as they moved up to the second place in line, behind a group of four teens with heads turned down toward hip level. They did not look long. Upon their departure was Jesus himself, lifeless and supine on a bed, in actual size, covered by a veil that heightened all of the features of his incredible face and hair and body. Jacoby gasped.

He had had a similar reaction when Helen took him to the Accademia in Florence to see "David" but that had more to do with the scope of the statue, the magnificence in all the grandeur and scale and expertise. The statue of the "Veiled Christ" was intimate. Beautiful. It felt to Jacoby like he was looking at a real person, and that real person was Jesus. Somehow the cloaking of the veil made it seem all the more real despite the magic of the accomplishment itself. Jacoby still didn't know if he believed in God, but he definitely now believed in Jesus. He was alive on the bed, under a marble veil.

Jacoby stared in wonder with no sense of time until Bill took him by the elbow and led him away through a collection of those waiting that extended back to the stairs. Jacoby didn't speak until they were on the street.

"Do you believe in God?" he asked Bill.

"I believe in man," Bill said. "But only sometimes."

Jacoby nodded, and the two of them walked off in search of a Neapolitan pizza and further testimony to mankind.

Chapter 24

In the historic center of Naples, they passed numerous places offering pizza, many busy with an early lunch crowd and some even with lines just outside the door. The air tingled with the scent of wood smoke and mineral-rich tomatoes roasting. Bill walked at a brisk clip, and Jacoby kept at his heels, anticipation rising from the aromas and culinary curiosity. All along, though, even back to when this pursuit began in Rome, Jacoby thought of it as kind of silly: It was only pizza. He hoped he was wrong.

Their pizzeria was tiny, off an empty street down a back alley. Bill stopped Jacoby out front and clasped his shoulders.

"Now," he said with patience. "It's important to recognize that the proprietors of this shop are a bunch of rude son of a bitches."

Jacoby smiled. "OK," he said with a nod.

"But we tolerate them and their, well, their intolerance because the pizza is sublime," Bill finished and took his hands from Jacoby's shoulders.

"Like Chick-fil-A," Jacoby said.

"Pardon?" Bill asked.

"Chick-fil-A," Jacoby continued. "You know. The fast food chicken place in the States."

"What of it?" Bill asked, his face turned and eyebrows knitted.

"They're famously homophobic," Jacoby said, "but even gay people eat there because the chicken sandwich is so good."

"Is it that good?" Bill asked.

"Got me," Jacoby said. "I don't eat fast food."

"Good boy," Bill said with a chuckle and led Jacoby inside the pizzeria.

The space was narrow and predictable in decor with white-tiled walls, wooden tables and chairs. The dining area was empty. Behind the glass counter, a pizzaiolo in white cap and white uniform had his face in the oven. He backed away from the heat with a bubbling pie on a peel. He slipped it on the counter, among the pizza-making configuration, and looked up with his red face.

"Oh, ciao!" he said with surprise and then enthusiasm to Bill. "Come stai?"

"Bene," Bill said with a polite nod and a gesture towards a nearby table. "Possiamo?"

"Sì. Sì. Vai," the man said with a flailing hand and confirmed the gesture by telling them to sit wherever they want. "Dove vuoi."

The man looked at Jacoby without saying anything and then turned his eyes back to Bill. He creased a quick smile and then walked briskly from behind the counter and out of sight.

"Seems nice to me," Jacoby said as they sat down.

Bill smirked and then drummed his fingers on the tabletop, searching the room for memories. The distinct smell excited Jacoby, and he began to believe the hype about pizza in Naples.

"What makes it so good?" Jacoby asked.

"Pardon?" Bill responded, shaken from his daydream.

"The pizza. What makes it so, you know, sublime?"

"I'd tell anybody else in the world the answer to that question," Bill said. "But I'm counting on you, my boy, to tell me."

"OK," Jacoby accepted the challenge. "I'll do my best."

Bill excused himself to the restroom, and Jacoby checked his phone for messages. The pizzaiolo returned with another man of the same age and attire. He could feel their stares from behind the counter. Jacoby looked up. "Ciao," he said.

"Ciao," the second man said back with a suspicious nod. "Americano?"

"Sì," Jacoby said sheepishly.

The man nodded and began an impassioned conversation with the other pizza maker that Jacoby could not make out. He tapped Voice Memo and put the phone on the table, curious about the Neapolitan dialect and the chance to translate on his own at some point, though he probably wouldn't. He was just killing time in Bill's absence and a little annoyed at being identified as an American after a single word of Italian.

When Bill returned the men stopped speaking; Jacoby turned off the recording and stood to take his turn washing up before lunch. "You order," he said to Bill and began walking toward the back.

"I'll wait," Bill said. "This happens very fast, and I don't want you to miss anything."

"OK," Jacoby said over his shoulder and picked up his step.

.　　.　　.

Bill gestured for Jacoby to join him at the counter. The pizzaioli were busy tending to the dough and feeding the oven wood, respectively. Bill asked for two different pizzas, and the men went to work on them. Oval balls of dough were worked into thin circles by fingertips on the flour-dusted counters of marble. Once on a peel, the dough was ladled with bright red sauce, which Jacoby could smell the minerals, and topped with Buffalo mozzarella pulled from a saltwater bath and shredded by hand. One pie was topped with sliced porcini mushroom. The men worked quickly and with great focus.

Bill looked at his watch as the pies entered the flaming oven. "Let's hold our breaths," he said to Jacoby.

"What?" Jacoby asked.

"It was a game Filippo and I would play," he said, his face flushed with a hint of red. "When waiting for our pizzas."

"Why?"

"Oh, just to be silly," Bill confessed. "And to acknowledge how quickly they cook."

"And how quickly is that?" Jacoby asked.

"You'll have to trust me," Bill said.

Jacoby shrugged and took a deep breath. Bill did the same. The pizzaioli gave them strange looks and went back to their busy work. After 30 seconds, Jacoby made wide eyes at Bill, who gave him an assured nod and then looked at the oven. A pizzaiolo, as if hearing an alarm, stopped needing dough and pulled the pizzas, one at a time, from the oven. Bill gusted out his breath, and Jacoby released his in relief. The plain pie took a handful of scattered basil leaves and both were quickly cut into quarters, plated and put on the counter. Bill nodded, asked for wine and water, and then took a plate to their table. Jacoby followed with the other. A waitress appeared from the back with a carafe of house red, a bottle of frizzante water, two plates, and four glasses.

"Eat the Margarita first," Bill said, motioning with his head toward the pie of sauce, cheese and basil. "It's the classic."

Bill filled their glasses and watched Jacoby shimmy free a slice and bring it to his mouth. There was a simultaneous encounter with texture and flavor, the toppings registering in concert with the snapping of the thin crust. It was an explosion of sorts. The disparate elements in perfect harmony. Jacoby chewed and swallowed slowly but not in an exaggerated manner; he fought the urge to devour the pizza in order to fully enjoy it at the proper pace. He put the charred crust on his plate.

"Well," Bill posed. "Honestly. What do you think?"

"Sublime," Jacoby said with a respectful nod.

Bill, pleased, nodded back and helped himself to a piece, taking the dangling cheese into his mouth before the tip of the slice. They ate the Margarita without speaking. There was banter from behind the counter and from other diners recently arrived. Jacoby kept busy figuring out the formula for perfection, and he had no trouble acknowledging the holy trinity of simplicity, ingredients, and execution. Easy enough, in Italy.

The mushroom pie was interesting to Jacoby, the earthiness adding a nice distinction, but he knew when Bill went back for a third pie it would be another Margarita. Jacoby held his breath and tasted basil.

Chapter 25

As the train whipped back toward Rome, Jacoby and Bill discussed dinner. Considering their three pizza lunch, it was decided that a light fish dinner would work or maybe some vegetarian fare. Jacoby wanted to go back to the wine bar in Trastevere for ceci pâté; Bill lobbied for an artichoke tasting menu in the Jewish ghetto.

In the midst of their negotiation, Bill's phone rang. Both men stopped speaking and exchanged concerned looks for a moment before Bill opened his phone and answered. "Pronto?"

Jacoby recognized Giovanni's voice, fast and loud, coming through the speaker. Bill held the phone away from his ear and pleaded with him to slow down. When Giovanni did so, Bill held the phone back to his ear and listened patiently, nodding and finally offering some very specific words in Italian of which Jacoby got the gist: Something had happened and one of them was going home.

"What happened?" Jacoby asked as soon as Bill had flipped his flip phone closed.

Bill took a breath and let it out. "It seems there's an issue with the hotel," he said.

"What kind of issue?" Jacoby answered. He had gotten used to a life without issues, and this was a jolt to his magical living.

"Something electrical," Bill said. "The power is out and one of us will need to be there to meet the electrician and arrange for payment."

"Can't Giovanni do it?" Jacoby asked.

"Perhaps," Bill said. "But I'd like one of us there just to be safe."

"I'll go," Jacoby said, happy to be of help and eager for the opportunity to see Helen and Boy. He missed them both.

"Would you mind?" Bill asked.

"Not at all," Jacoby said.

Bill nodded, pulled his mouth and looked away. His face looked wan, and Jacoby considered how important the hotel was to Bill on so many levels. He would be sure to get this straightened out and prove his worth as a partner. It would also be a good opportunity to work on his Italian, though he'd have Giovanni along as an interpreter. An announcement was made that the train was arriving soon in Rome.

"I'll be in touch with the electrician," Bill said. "Just go straight to the hotel or the bar when you get home."

"Now?" Jacoby asked. "I'm going now?"

"Yes," Bill said. "The next stop on this train is Florence, so you might as well just stay on board."

"What about my things?"

"They will be fine," Bill assured him. "And you will be back for them on Monday."

"OK," Jacoby said with a shrug. "Cool."

He took out his phone to text Helen that he would be home that night.

·   ·   ·

Bill got off in Rome, and Jacoby grew restless. The mid-afternoon sun was holding steady at its apex for the day, and he hoped to have the issue with the hotel resolved with enough time to get back into Florence. He also wanted to see Boy, which might be cruel to do so only in passing. He texted Helen again, asked her to meet him at the train station and come out to Antella for the night. They would stay for two nights in the barn with the dog and return together to Florence on Monday morning where Jacoby would catch his train back to Rome. Helen agreed, and Jacoby relaxed, feeling like everything was in order. He took out his phone to keep busy, to practice translating some of the conversations he'd recorded, but his battery was low. So he placed his hands on his lap and made like Bill in his cat nap pose. Jacoby drifted off and woke when the train rattled and hissed into the station at Santa Maria Novella.

Helen was on the platform, in the natural light, a gray fedora covering her blond bob, her lithe frame in a sleeveless black sweater over black leather pants and white shoes for walking. An overnight bag and a light jacket hung over her arm.

"Get a load of you," Jacoby said, smiling as he hurried toward her.

Helen demurred in a playful way, posing from side to side. 'I'm a movie star on vacation," she said. "And it is Saturday, after all."

She clutched her arms behind Jacoby's neck and pecked him hard on the lips. Her hat tipped to the side, and it stayed ajar until they finished their embrace. "I hope we can get a table at Antella's finest ristorante," Jacoby joked.

"My god," Helen gushed. "I hadn't thought of that. Where will we take our dinner?"

"Don't worry," Jacoby said. "We can pick something up at the butcher and eat at home."

"Oooh," Helen cooed. "I could go for a thick bistecca fiorentina."

"Me, too," Jacoby said, shaking his head. "I've been eating cucina Romana all week."

"Poor baby," Helen said and made a rosebud of her lips.

"But we better hurry," Jacoby pointed out. "Before he closes."

Helen handed Jacoby her travel bag and hooked her arm inside his. They quick-stepped in tandem through the station and into the shimmering light out front where a taxi warbled up and picked up two passengers on their way to the village of Antella in the hills just south of Florence.

Chapter 26

The cab pulled up in front of the hotel, and Jacoby immediately knew something was very wrong. Giovanni was pacing out front, biting his nails, running a hand through his tangled hair. There was no electrician. The slam of the car door turned Giovanni's head, and he bolted for Jacoby with his hands up. "Mi dispiace," he said, thumping his chest. "Mi dispiace."

"What happened?" Jacoby asked, fear coursing through him along with potentially awful scenarios. "What happened?"

Giovanni stopped arms distance from Jacoby and tried to speak slowly, but his words were rambling and too frantic to translate. The only word beyond the apologies that he understood was "cane" and that was bad because cane meant dog, and Jacoby knew it was in reference to his dog. Helen came up behind Jacoby and put her hand inside his elbow. "My god," she gasped. "What is going on?"

"I don't know," Jacoby said quickly without taking his eyes from Giovanni. "I don't know what the fuck he's saying except that it has something to do with my dog."

Jacoby clenched his teeth and stared furiously at Giovanni who was reduced to a pantomime of apologies. Helen clapped to get Giovanni's attention and then put up her hands in a calming fashion. "Piano," she asked him slowly to slow down and then to tell her what happened. "Dimmi cosa è successo?"

Giovanni turned to Helen, took a big breath and clasped his palms in praying motion. His hands were shaking, but he was able to communicate the story clearly enough to Helen, though Jacoby, with Giovanni speaking at a reduced clip, was able to understand: The hunters had taken his dog.

"I get it," he said to Helen when she turned to offer the translation. "The hunters took my dog back."

"I'm confused," Helen said to Jacoby. "How did their dog become your dog?"

He'd never completely explained to Helen the circumstances that led to Boy becoming his beyond the animal being a gift, of sorts, from Nicoletta. It really wasn't hers to give him, as the dog belonged to her husband, the hunter, but his abusiveness towards his wife and his dog had led them, respectively, to Giovanni and Jacoby.

"I'll tell you later," he said to Helen and turned to Giovanni. "Dove?" he asked him where they were. Jacoby had calmed himself somewhat and knew that Giovanni was not to blame; in fact, he suspected he would need Giovanni's help in whatever his plan would be to retrieve Boy.

"Non so," Giovanni shrugged. "Probabilmente a casa, sulle colline."

"Tu sai dove?" Jacoby asked Giovanni if he knew where that was.

Giovanni shook his head and pointed to the cafe.

"OK," Jacoby said and walked off toward the cafe to talk to Nicoletta.

"Where are you going?" Helen asked.

"Come on," Jacoby called back to her. "I'm going to need your help."

Nicoletta was out front with a forlorn look and her arms folded under her chest. Her lips pursed into a rosebud as Jacoby approached. He held up a hand when her mouth opened to surely utter an apology. "It's OK," he said to her. "It's OK."

Helen and Giovanni joined the foursome. Jacoby apologized and introduced Helen to his two Italian friends. "Oh," Helen chirped. "The ones from the sagra!"

"Yeah," Jacoby said.

Helen spoke to them in rapid, friendly Italian, and the three, it seemed to Jacoby, were fast friends. Jacoby interrupted and asked Helen to ask Nicoletta how to find the hunter's house. He also asked for an explanation of the property and where the dog would most likely be kept. Nicoletta nodded and explained it to Helen who shared with Jacoby.

"Capisci?" Jacoby asked Giovanni if he understood.

Giovanni nodded confidently.

"OK," Jacoby said to him. "Andiamo."

The two men walked off into the piazza.

"Where are you going now?" Helen called.

"To the hunter's house in the hills to get my dog," he answered while angling toward the butcher shop.

.   .   .

Helen met Jacoby outside the butcher when he came out and accompanied him to the motorino parked in front of the hotel. She had wanted to come, but Jacoby begged her to stay in the cafe with Nicoletta. She reluctantly agreed after gauging Jacoby's urgency. "Be brave," she said to him as he boarded Bill's motorino, "but not stupid."

"Come on," he said with a confident smile. "I once killed a cinghiale with an ax."

"You mention that a lot, you know?" Helen said with a smirk.

Jacoby pointed at his face and slowly mouthed "Killed a cinghiale with an ax."

Helen shook her head, and Jacoby handed her one of the two packages he'd procured from the butcher. "What's this?" she asked.

"Your bistecca, my dear." he said. "We'll have it once I get back from being brave but not stupid."

"Very good," she said. "I'll take good care of it in your absence."

"Have Nicoletta put it in one of her coolers," Jacoby advised.

"I will!" Helen insisted. "Now go, already!"

Jacoby flipped the face mask of his helmet down, started the motorino and pulled up behind Giovanni who had been waiting in his old Fiat. They went out of the village in the direction of the barn, on the two-lane road boarded by olive groves. At the top of a hill, where the road T's out, where Jacoby takes a left on the ridge to go home, they went right. The road rose dramatically and twisted among a smattering of small, spreading homes set back off the street. Dusk settled and the sun smoldered beyond the mountains to the west, casting an orange glow on the tree-line in the distance. Bugs bounced off Jacoby's mask and stuck to his neck. The Fiat's lights went on and Jacoby followed safely behind, his heart beating against the small package tucked into his shirt.

The hazard lights for the Fiat went on, and Giovanni's arm hooked out of the window to point at a pink house to the right. Jacoby could hear the dog barking as he passed. He followed the Fiat for 100 yards until Giovanni found a space on the shoulder of the road to pull over. Jacoby pulled up next to the driver's side and removed the package of meat scraps he had procured from the butcher. He gave it to Giovanni and reminded him of their plan. It was daring, no doubt, but Jacoby would put himself in harm's way for his dog. He already had, having saved the animal from the tusks of the ferocious cinghiale.

Jacoby watched Giovanni walk the side of the road, and he waited until the shoemaker settled in a thicket of hedge beside the house. Jacoby turned the motorino around and returned to the pink house. He parked it in the yard near the road. When he turned off the engine, the sound of the barking dog increased. The backyard of dirt was fenced in by chicken wire and poorly lit by a single light. Boy must have smelled Jacoby, and his barks turned into whimpers. He sounded so desperate, so needy, and the dog clearly strained against a leash. Jacoby's heart broke and his anger rose as he walked the front yard of crabgrass, rocks, and dirt patches to the screen door. Sounds of a soccer game came from a TV in a room in the back of the house lit only by blue light. Jacoby clenched his fists and took a breath, slowly in and out through his nose, before knocking on the screen door, hard enough for Giovanni to hear. When Jacoby backed away from the door into the small front yard, gravel crunched under his feet.

Voices immediately rose, and feet trampled the floorboards. Jacoby hoped the hunter would be home alone, but three figures came from the back, with Nicoletta's husband leading the way in a V formation. He had a cigarette stuck straight in his mouth like a lollipop, his brown curls dangling on the shoulder strap of his sleeveless t-shirt; suspenders hung down along his khakis to where they met knee-high rubber boots. He pushed open the screen door and came on to the cement porch where he stood, tall and broad and handsome. He motioned with his hand behind him, and the two other men stayed in the shadows within the doorway, arms crossed and scowling.

"Give me my fucking dog," Jacoby said, his attempts at sounding fierce belied by the currency of his fear and desperation. His voice cracked in the middle of the profanity.

The hunter laughed and threw his lit cigarette at Jacoby's feet. "It's my dog," he said in slow, ugly English, poking his own chest with bunched fingertips.

"Let's fight for him," Jacoby said with raised fists.

The hunter huffed, cracked a crooked smile and tilted his head. "You want to fight with me for the dog?" he asked slowly, in broken phrases.

"Yes!" Jacoby said with an emphatic nod.

The hunter shrugged. "OK," he said. "Perchè no?"

When the hunter stepped into the yard, Jacoby noted that the dog had stopped barking. He braced himself in the set position he had learned during his limited study of martial arts and delivered his signature move, a kick to the sternum of the approaching combatant. The hunter fell onto his back in the dirt on the concrete landing. Jacoby bolted for the motorino as the screen door slammed. The two other men caught him boarding the motorino and each grabbed an arm, twisting it behind Jacoby's back. Pain tore through his shoulders, and the smell of the men, of wine and smoke and body odor, filled his nose. His heart was pounding and his pores opened down his neck and back. Jacoby struggled to get free, but both men were bigger and stronger.

The hunter moseyed up, rubbing his sternum. Jacoby held up his chin in defiance, and the hunter punched him in the face. Jacoby's nose oozed, and he could smell the blood before it spilled over his lips and into his mouth, tasting of dirt and copper. He slumped, but the men straightened him back up. The next punch, a hook, landed over his eye, and Jacoby saw black. When vision returned it was blurry, and he hardly saw the hunter rear back to deliver a straight blow to his chin. This sent Jacoby flailing, and the men let him fall into the undergrowth, the nettles and rocks and weeds scraping up the back of his lifted shirt. Jacoby felt itchy and dizzy and sick to his stomach. He rolled over and thought he might vomit, and the thought entered his mind that the men might kill him and that he should run while he had a chance, but they started talking among themselves in a tone that sounded congratulatory, spiked with laughter. Someone kicked him in the side.

"My dog," the hunter barked at Jacoby.

There was the sound of spitting, but Jacoby didn't feel anything. As their boots scuffled the ground toward the house, Jacoby hurried to his feet, and despite the pain and disorientation, he got on the motorino, started it with shaking hands and retreated down the hill toward the village where his dog would be waiting.

Chapter 27

Jacoby drove carefully and as fast as he could down the hill and around the final bend for the piazza. He hadn't bothered to put on the helmet, and bugs bounced off his face and the blood under his nose dried and flaked off. Upon the piazza, he hopped the curb, rode across the dimpled surface and dumped the motorino on its side in front of the cafe. His friends were out front waiting for him. Boy leapt from Nicoletta's arms and bound for Jacoby. Jacoby fell to his knees and hugged his dog, petting him furiously around the head and neck. Boy licked the dried blood and sweat and bug smatterings from his face.

"My god," Helen said. "Look at your face."

Jacoby looked up at her and smiled. "I guess a kiss is out of the question?" he asked.

"Kiss you? I can hardly stand to look at you!" She put her hands on her hips and made an exasperated face. "What part of brave not stupid did you not understand?"

Jacoby ignored her and continued petting his dog, registering the pain around his face and acknowledging its worth. Helen squatted down to pet the dog and inspect Jacoby's wounds. She brushed back his bangs and kissed him gently on the forehead. Giovanni and Nicoletta stood nearby, arms around each other's shoulders, smiling.

"That was pretty clever, to lure the dog away with the meat scraps," Helen admitted.

"Thanks," Jacoby said and raised his chin. "That was the smart part."

"And the stupid part was turning yourself into a punching bag as a distraction," Helen added.

Jacoby nodded and nuzzled Boy whose breath smelled of meat scraps. "Hey," he said to Helen. "Where's our steak?"

Helen shook her head and motioned toward the cafe.

"Let's go!"

Instead of going back to the barn, Jacoby opened up the hotel and made plans to stay the night. He had clean clothes there, and toiletries were available. Helen found the hotel charming, and she waited on the back terrace with Boy while Jacoby showered and tended to his wounds. Jacoby was willing to break Bill's rule about the dog in the hotel on this occasion, but he thought to at least keep him out back as much as possible. The thought of Bill had reminded Jacoby of the clever manner in which his friend had tricked him back to the village without having him worried sick the entire train ride. That would have been torture, and Jacoby was happy to call Bill in Rome to thank him for that and to let him know how things had turned out. Bill was gracious, of course, and relieved by the outcome. He also suggested that Jacoby not return to Rome and stay around the village to protect the dog and the hotel in case of the hunters' return. Jacoby agreed and hurried out back to join Helen and Boy with the good news.

Jacoby's battered face didn't hurt as bad as it looked, and he was in high spirits after cleaning up and applying some ice. He was especially uplifted, after coming through the sliding doors onto the slate terrace, by the sight of his lover and his dog bonding beneath Tuscan stars.

Boy left Helen's side and did circles around Jacoby's legs as he crossed the surface to join Helen at the table under the wisteria trellis. The still and cool air soothed Jacoby as did the reality of the night's events. It wasn't lost on him how Italy somehow inspired a heroism that he'd never had before. It reminded him, once again, of the surprising admiration Helen had for the calcio storico, the ancient and annual game of Florence she had taken him to on their first and impromptu date. The match was a bloody, nearly ruleless affair that was hard to watch, but Helen thought of it as heroic as the men, the calciente, put themselves in harm's way to defend their own.

"Hey," Jacoby suggested as he approached. "Maybe I should go out for the calcio storico next year?"

Helen laughed. "Please," she said through a hand that covered her mouth. "You'd get slaughtered."

He squeezed into the wrought iron chair where Helen sat. "Yeah, maybe," he admitted.

Helen brushed his bangs away and inspected his face. "You can take a punch, though."

"I've got that going for me," Jacoby conceded with a contrite smile. "I'm also done with my Roman adventure."

"What?" Helen asked, sitting up. "You're not going back to Rome?"

"I guess not," Jacoby said. "Bill said he's coming home in a few days, and he wants me to be sure we're ready for the event at the consortium."

"And when is that again?" Helen asked.

"Next Saturday."

"Looks like you've got a busy week ahead of you, doesn't it?" Helen said.

"Yeah," Jacoby sighed. "I guess I do."

"Well then," Helen decided. "We better make the most of tonight."

. . .

Helen whipped up some spritzes at the bar inside while Jacoby stoked the logs within the barbeque pit he and Bill had built from bricks over the summer. When the flames were licking the metal grate, Jacoby stepped carefully into the garden for some vine tomatoes and basil. He also ripped a thick branch of rosemary from the shrub along the wall.

The steak was seasoned with salt and pepper and left on the wheeled butcher's block aside the grill. Boy sat on his haunches next to the butcher's block, licking his chops and staring intently.

"Don't worry, Boy," Jacoby said as he prodded the logs. "You'll be getting plenty of meat tonight."

Helen came outside carefully carrying two large glasses of sparkling colors. She handed one to Jacoby and produced a bottle of wine that had been stuck in her back pocket. "I thought this would do," she said, presenting a bottle of Sassicaia.

"Oooh," Jacoby cooed. "A Super Tuscan. Nice call."

Helen put the bottle next to the meat and held up her glass, and Jacoby did the same. "To you," Helen said. "My very own Super Tuscan in the flesh."

Jacoby laughed. "Speaking of flesh," he said. "Let's get this steak going."

While the meat seared and the smell rose from the grill, Jacoby chopped the tomatoes, scraping the juice and seeds back into the garden. From under the block, he produced unmarked bottles of olive oil and vinegar, both local. He made a quick vinaigrette in a ceramic bowl and added the tomatoes. After turning the steak, he tore shreds of basil over the bowl of tomatoes and tossed the ingredients by pulling the bowl toward him numerous times. The tomatoes rose in a wave and curled back into the bowl.

"Stop showing off," Helen said from the chair she had dragged near the grill.

"I can't," Jacoby said over his shoulder. "I'm Super Tuscan."

"Oh for god's sake," Helen cried. "I should have never put the idea in your head."

"You know, as we sit here," Jacoby quipped, testing the steak with a finger. "I'm just thinking about what my uniform is going to look like."

"That's it," Helen said and stood. "I'm making myself another drink. Would you like one?"

"Super Tuscan says 'Yes,'" Jacoby said in a serious voice, using the 3rd person, without turning around. He smiled at the sound of Helen's exasperated cackle as she went inside the hotel.

When she returned the steak was resting on the butcher's block, emitting ripples of heat and leaking a tiny bit of juice. Jacoby warmed the rosemary branch over the flames and minced the stripped needles, then he halved a lemon. Jacoby sipped his spritz and squinted playfully at Helen who looked away, refusing to carry on the 'Super Tuscan' charade. Jacoby carved the filet mignon side of the bistecca and put it all in Boy's bowl. The dog gobbled it up as Jacoby carefully removed the strip side from the bone. He trimmed some fat along the edges and then cut the meat against the bias into succulent, pink slices that glistened with rising juice. He layered them neatly on the board, after wiping away excess juices, and sprinkled the meat with coarse salt, fresh ground pepper, the minced rosemary and a squeeze of lemon. He dumped the tomatoes beside the meat and wheeled the butcher's block beneath the wisteria.

Helen came over, trying to hide that she was impressed.

"Well," Jacoby cajoled. "What do you think."

Helen crossed her arms.

"Say it," Jacoby teased, stepping in front of the sumptuous presentation. "Say it..."

Helen blew at her bangs and rolled her eyes. "Fine," she said. "You win. It looks super."

"Super...Tuscan," Jacoby said with a nod. "Now we can eat."

Chapter 28

The steak was spectacular, full of flavor and tender in texture within the crusted exterior. The giant, round wine was the perfect compliment with much fruit up front and depth on the finish. They ate slowly, enjoying the tomatoes as a zesty side. After cleaning up, they brought Boy into the front salon, to keep any trace of fur out of a guest room, where they slept on the pullout sofa with the dog between them.

In the morning, they took a pastry and cappuccino at the cafe under the awning out front and watched the piazza come to life. Many of the villagers, passing on their way to the first church service of the morning, nodded in reverence or said "Buongiorno, Jake!"

"You're quite the celebrity," Helen acknowledged.

Jacoby pointed at his face and was about to mouth his refrain about killing the cinghiale, but Helen waved him off before he could begin. As the church bells rang, Jacoby fed Boy the rest of his pastry and went inside for Giovanni's car keys. Not wanting to risk Boy with Giovanni and Nicoletta, or expose them to risk as well should the hunters return that morning, he borrowed the Fiat, took Helen's travel bag, and brought Boy and the bag home to the barn.

Paolo was in his trees, along with a crew of laborers, gathering olives from his grove. He climbed down to greet Jacoby, who told him what had happened with the hunters. Paolo looked concerned, and he suggested Jacoby come by that night for dinner and a conversation about the upcoming celebration at the consortium. Jacoby agreed, with particular enthusiasm after being informed of the menu, and asked if Paolo would keep an eye on Boy while he was away. He hated to leave the dog, but the barn door was open, and Boy would surely have a full day running around the grove and roaming the property while Jacoby and Helen went off on a Tuscan excursion.

The sun was shining as it had pretty much everyday since Jacoby had arrived in Italy the previous spring. He was particularly fond of the autumn sunshine which had a lemony tinge that reminded him of egg yolks. He started the motorino, and Helen hopped on back, latching her arms around his rib cage. They puttered out of the village on a one-way access road and through the sparse countryside where they soon turned onto the northern tip of the Chiantigiana Highway, the fabled two-lane that connected the cities of Florence and Siena. Of all the excursions in Tuscany, this day trip and visits to Florence were his favorites.

The initial stretch of this roadway was no indication of the magnificence that lie ahead, and Jacoby always thought of it as a burden to pass, either coming or going, through such prosaic scenery on a motorino that couldn't do more than 30 miles per hour, even less so with a passenger on back. But soon enough the countryside opened up, and the motorino leaned and weaved with the turns past enormous, verdant pastures spotted with white cows and fields covered in oceans of wild flowers.

The topography increased in height, and the hills were lined with olive trees and ancient vines bursting with grapes not yet harvested. Jacoby breathed in their ripeness and could detect the musky odor of grapes trampled in the process and returned to the earth. He grew hungry and eager for lunch as they entered the heart of Chianti country. They swept past the first tourist town, Greve-in-Chianti, and Jacoby thought that maybe he'd change his name to Jacoby-in-Chianti if he didn't go with Super Tuscan. He made a note to ask Helen about this over lunch. She was so cute when bemused.

·   ·   ·

The full majesty of the area arrived after a steep and winding climb to the town of Panzano. The town itself was merely a crossroad, and they passed through toward the swimming pool sky that stretched above the radiant valley and august hills. Jacoby steered the motorino off the Chiantigiana Highway onto a narrow, shaded road boarded tightly on both sides by woods and gorse. The reprieve from the sunlight felt good, but the bug factor picked up. Helen scrunched her head behind Jacoby's neck to keep the insects from splattering on her face mask. Cobwebs clung to his forearms and neck.

The sunlight returned as did Helen's face over Jacoby's right shoulder. He pointed up toward the walled-in city of Radda-in-Chianti just before turning onto another rural road marked by a sign for Volpaia. The shaded road passed industrial flatlands and a corrugated, tin-roofed structure where men were busy unloading olives or grapes from the bed of three-wheeled vehicles. Once in the sunshine, the road rose sharply and carved through vineyards and olive groves on steep slopes lined with Cypress trees. The crisp air smelled of herbs and the fruit being collected by men in the fields. Jacoby's ears popped as they climbed toward the small circle of rooflines below the sky.

Just below the village's lofted entrance, Jacoby curled around a circular road bordered on one side by a massive wall. The valley to the other side was full of breadth and sunshine and color. Helen rubbed Jacoby's shoulders in excitement, and he was so happy to have introduced her to a new place in Tuscany. They bumped along a dirt and gravel track, the tires making a popping sound on the stones. Jacoby cut the engine and relished the relief of the silent engine. He cleared his ears as Helen climbed off and looked over the direction from which they had come, a yawning expanse of rolling green shades.

"It just never fails to amaze me," she said. "How staggering the beauty is here."

Jacoby took off his helmet, stretched and stood beside her. "Oh my god," he said with mock-astonishment. "I hadn't noticed."

Helen shoved him with her shoulder, and they walked off, arm in arm, toward the tiny village.

The tour of the circular village perimeter was fast and charming. There were little doors and windows among the stone facades with flower boxes along their base. Tiny stairways where cats milled and lounged. Many of the building's interiors were open to passersby who could watch the men and women working the apparatuses for local production which perfumed the air with an unctuous musk. Beyond every lane was the glowing valley.

After the quick turn, Jacoby and Helen returned to the entrance of the village, a town square of sorts with some shops selling local products, a cafe, and a few eateries. They took a table on the terrace of La Bottega, draped in greenery, and had their lunch under a canopy overlooking a postcard panorama that was almost surreal in its expanse and gorgeousness.

They shared crostini with chicken liver pâté and fried zucchini blossoms stuffed with fresh ricotta for antipasti, and then a primo piatti of squash ravioli in a sage, brown butter sauce. Their secondi was guinea hen roasted with cippolini onions in a perfume of the town's wine which they had been sipping all along. Helen had a chocolate tart for dessert and Jacoby took a small grappa. They walked the village again after lunch and bought a bottle of the Volpaia Chianti Classico Riserva and a bottle of the local olive oil. Then they got back on the motorino and headed for home.

Chapter 29

The Tuscan sun was an orange orb in the pristine sky, hanging at its apex in mid-afternoon as Jacoby and Helen puttered back along the Chiantigiana Highway. Every time a car, motorcycle or even the occasional group of particularly competitive bicyclists, passed them, Jacoby clenched his teeth and dreamed of the day when he could practice the speed so embraced by Italians. Oh, how he would love to get from place to place at greater velocity, though he was able to appreciate the pacing and, of course, the ability at all to get around provided by Bill's rusty motorino.

Without access to the motorino, Jacoby would not have been able to take Helen into Chianti country and then back through the village and eventually up to the barn in the hills where he lived. It was late afternoon, and the shadows were long across the valley as they came up the bumpy track to Paolo's property from where a pine-and-rosemary scented plume of smoke rose from behind his villa roof of Spanish tiles. Jacoby and Helen passed through the electronic fence and parked in the carport. Boy was already bounding through the olive grove by the time Jacoby reached the terrace on the other side of the barn. The dog nearly tumbled down the twisted, narrow staircase that connected the terrace and grove.

"Good, Boy. Good, Boy," Jacoby said as he squatted down to pet his beloved companion that keened and yelped and shimmied with joy. The power of a dog's love was always a reminder and validation to

Jacoby of the wonder of being alive. And this reminded Jacoby of another of life's blessings. "Let's get you some food, Boy."

Inside the barn, Jacoby fed Boy some of the chicken and rice mixture he made in advance as Helen inspected the barn. She, predictably, found it charming and declared so after scaling the spiral staircase that led to the loft-like bedroom upstairs. "Join me for a shower," she called down to Jacoby. He took Boy's half-finished bowl, along with some water, into the side room on the ground floor. Boy whimpered as Jacoby closed the door, but he knew he'd be fast asleep on the couch after a long day outside and a hearty meal.

Jacoby joined Helen upstairs in the shower and then in the bed with the doors open to the Juliet balcony and the breeze tousling the parted curtains. The grove was empty, and Jacoby knew that Paolo was next door tending to their dinner, stoking the flames of his outdoor forno with wood Jacoby chopped in the shed beyond the barn as well as the branches of rosemary Paolo snapped from the hedge within his fence.

.   .   .

After a quick nap, Jacoby dressed in jeans and a black T-shirt and went next door. Helen was asked to join, but she didn't feel like eating the type of meal Jacoby had described as Paolo's speciality, and she also had some messages to send regarding tours the next morning. She was happy to stay home with Boy in the lovely barn and go to sleep early. Jacoby understood, but he also missed her as soon as he rang Paolo's bell and the sound of the screen door slammed from behind the villa.

"Come. Come," Paolo said after opening the fence door, his bald head and face brown and spotted from all of the time outside. He had on a tweed work shirt and olive-stained khakis. He looked tired but had enthusiasm in his gestures, happy for a harvest that he thought wouldn't come. While many of the villagers appreciated Jacoby for the cinghiale episode, Paolo was far more grateful for the fact that Jacoby had connected him and his cronies with Dolores, who provided the necessary funds to purchase the consortium and continue with the village's collective production of olive oil and wine.

And some of that wine, from a previous harvest, was on the shaded table in Paolo's large, terra-cotta floored terrace bordered by potted lemon trees, various plants, and a massive hedge of rosemary. "Pronto?" Paolo asked. "Ready to make the pizza?"

Jacoby followed Paolo to the forno and settled beside him at the marble counter where two balls of dough rested on a flour-dusted surface. Heat emanated from the oven, and Jacoby smelled the covered tin of roasted meat tucked into the farthest corner from the flames. His jowls, like always, were sluiced with saliva in anticipation for the misto arrosto, the mixed roast that was among Jacoby's favorite staples of cucina tipica. But first, they had to make the pizza, which was Paolo's tradition and something Jacoby knew he could never avoid. He liked Paolo's pizza and was enjoying learning how to make his own, but he didn't think the misto arrosto needed an appetizer.

Jacoby picked up his ball of dough and slapped the topside down into the flour. He slapped it around some more, from side to side until it stretched enough for shaping. Back on the marble he worked it out with his fingertips, pulling at times, into a rounded shape, making sure to rotate the dough to avoid sticking. He repaired a small tear, firmed up the outer edges and looked to Paolo who had finished a moment before. "Very good," Paolo said. "You are becoming a fine pizzaiolo."

"Grazie," Jacoby said.

The hard part was over, and all Jacoby had to do was not oversauce the dough, and the rest would be a breeze, until the launch. On more than one occasion, Jacoby's attempt at getting the assembled pie off the peel had resulted in an aborted attempt, at which Paolo would make him start over. Jacoby hated that. He made sure that his peel was thoroughly dusted before slipping the pie on top. He shimmied the peel to confirm the pie would move, and then he carried it to the front of the oven and quickly plunged in the peel and pulled it back with a confident tug, leaving the pie on the scalding surface in front of the dancing flames.

Jacoby watched his pizza cook, the crust firming and the cheese melting. He thought of the pizzaioli in Naples and remembered their conversation he had recorded. When he and Paolo sat to eat their pizza he took out his phone and played the Voice Memo, asking Paolo to translate.

"I can not," Paolo said through a full mouth.

"Perchè no?" Jacoby asked.

"Because," Paolo said and paused before continuing. "It is not Italian."

"What is it?"

"Dialect of some sort," Paolo said with a shrug. "Probabilmente napoletano."

"That's not Italian?" Jacoby asked, annoyed and bemused by the snobbish provincialism that existed in Italy, especially the upper class Florentines like Paolo.

"No," Paolo said and drank some of the local wine, which was the only wine he drank.

Jacoby knew better than to pursue this, so he ate his pizza and washed it down with the local wine, which - regardless of Paolo's gross subjectivity - was very good. He was looking forward to the increased production and distribution of this year's harvest and beyond afforded by Dolores' infusion of cash and business acumen.

"So," Paolo broached after both pizzas were eaten. "The event next weekend is very important."

"I know," Jacoby said, already aware of where this conversation was going.

"I know these hunters for many, many years," he said. "They always make trouble for the village. They are not really one with us, in many ways."

Jacoby nodded and thought about what douchebags they must have been in high school as Paolo refilled their wine glasses. "And I, we, have concern," he continued, "that they will make problems for us at the festival."

Jacoby inferred, by the way Paolo was looking at the marks on his face, that he felt Jacoby was somewhat responsible for the increased threat. This annoyed him, as did the onus put on him all along to make sure the harvest festival was a success. Dolores asked him to keep an eye on things, but Paolo and company asked him to do everything, as if he worked for them. Jacoby had already arranged for the catering from the village butcher, and now, it seemed, he was tasked with providing security as well.

"What do you want me to do?" Jacoby asked.

"I don't know," Paolo said and flattened his lips. "Something."

Paolo got up to get the misto arrosto from the forno, and Jacoby fretted over another rematch with the hunters. The whole thing was ridiculous, and he just wanted it to go away on its own, though he knew that things like this rarely did. His consternation was interrupted by the return of Paolo with a tin container held in mitted hands. Paolo removed the foil seal to a whoosh of steam perfumed by aromatics and juice and fat. He dumped the contents onto a ceramic platter and seasoned it aggressively with coarse salt. After a swirl of local olive oil and the stripping of a fresh rosemary stem, they were ready to eat.

Per Paolo's invitation, Jacoby loaded his plate first with pieces of roasted lamb, sausage, rabbit, liver in caul fat, guinea hen, halved-potatoes, a halved head of garlic, caramelized carrot and fennel. It was the same thing every time, and Jacoby suspected it was a meal of which he would never grow tired. The array of flavors and textures and aromas were simply too satisfying. While Paolo helped himself, Jacoby tore a piece of bread from a loaf, wiped it in the bottom of the tin and squeezed some of the roasted garlic gloves out from the soft head, thinking he could live on the drippings, roasted garlic and bread alone.

Paolo held up his glass. "Salute," he said. "And to the health of the festival also."

Jacoby tapped his glass into Paolo's, took a quick sip of the wine and dug into the misto arrosto, allowing the pleasure of eating to distract him from the looming problem he'd have to face.

Chapter 30

With Helen back in Florence, Jacoby got to work at his station in the hotel, a desk set up in the front parlor by the window that looked over the piazza. There was lots of follow up to do regarding the festival, particularly reminders via email to those local media figures and influencers who had expressed potential interest in coming or had confirmed attendance. Jacoby recognized that even expats in Italy adopted a nonchalance about commitment and getting things done that resembled the Italian ethos. Still, he was confident in the turnout as there did seem to be genuine enthusiasm for the event which offered a new variety of Chianti from the Florence microregion and a new place to lodge so close to the city yet remote and unfettered by tourism. Jacoby was also excited to meet many of the special guests, both expats and Italians, as they seemed like his kind of people.

The bigger issue involved getting those from the city out to the event and back. Most city dwellers didn't own cars, and even those with motorinos might balk at having to get out to new terrain and then home again after a day of eating and drinking. Public transportation sucked from the city, and Jacoby needed to arrange a private bus, which was no easy task considering his limited resources and lack of language. He had asked Helen for her help, and she promised to look into it with locals she knew in Florence who provided private bus tours of Tuscany.

By lunch, Jacoby was feeling good about things. The process of launching a new business and helping with that of another filled him with a type of entrepreneurial spirit he'd never had. And this unexpected career move into hospitality, abetted by his experience in PR, was proving to be his calling. He phoned Bill to offer the promising update and check on his progress, but the call went directly to voicemail. He didn't leave a message and vowed to try again after lunch.

The cafe tables under the awning had some local elders arguing about soccer and a collection of harvest workers taking up two tables and taking, with spoons, Nicoletta's cheap and filling daily lunch special from large ceramic bowls. Jacoby greeted her as he passed through the empty barroom and into the small area in back where he was alone in the diffuse light. He took his lunch there almost every day, and he enjoyed speaking measured Italian with Nicoletta as she practiced with him a simple Italian devoid of her Neapolitan dialect. It was, in some ways, like they were learning the language together. Jacoby checked his phone as Nicoletta approached to say hello and take his order.

"Ciao, americano," she said, and then asked how he was. "Come va? Tutto bene?"

"Tutto a posto," he answered, letting her know, through one of his favorite Italian colloquialisms, that 'all was in place,' before asking the day's lunch special. "Che c'è per il pranzo oggi?"

"Ah," Nicoletta said with a look of satisfaction on her face. "Ribollita, la mia preferita." She twisted her forefinger into one of her pillowy cheeks and rolled her eyes in mock-ecstacy.

"Perfetto," Jacoby responded and rubbed his hands together.

Jacoby was happy about the Tuscan bread soup for lunch because it was exceptional and lighter than the heavy fare he'd been indulging in as of late; he was also hungry, and the soup, already prepared, arrived quickly with a half-carafe of local red, a bottle of acqua frizzante, salt in a ramekin, and a bottle of local oil. Nicoletta filled his wine glass and hurried back up front to take care of the other guests. Her status saddened Jacoby. Even though she was liberated from her husband physically, she had no other choice but to continue doing all the work at his family's bar for what Jacoby had to assume was very little pay. She worked entirely alone and extraordinarily hard. Every day.

Jacoby and Nicoletta had a careful, polite relationship, similar to the one she had with Bill, as all three were strangers in the village, her having come from Naples a few years back to marry the hunter and run his family's bar. Jacoby had been privy to the secret of her affair with Giovanni, and he had also played a large role in their affair becoming public, which left her estranged from her malevolent husband and more connected to the rest of the village, particularly the strangers from America.

Jacoby was thinking of Nicoletta as he spooned mouthfuls of her hearty soup stocked with white beans, tomatoes, zucchini, carrots, shredded cabbage and softened, day-old bread. The broth was opaque and full of flavor enhanced by the salt and fresh oil. The versatile wine of the town paired with vegetable dishes as well as it stood up to roasted or grilled meats. Jacoby felt nourished by the healthy meal, and he meant to pay his compliments to Nicoletta as she approached, but an idea suddenly came to him.

"Nicoletta," Jacoby broached. "Sei di Napoli, no?"

"Sì," she said.

"E c'è una differente lingua lì?" he asked about the different dialect to which Paolo had referred.

"Sì," she said, squinting in curiosity or defensiveness. "Ma, non molto differente."

"Io so. Io so," Jacoby let her know that he knew and understood. "Capisco."

"Perché?" Nicoletta asked why as Jacoby thumbed through his phone.

Jacoby held up a hand to ask her patience and offered her a seat. There was noise from the front of the barroom, and Nicoletta went to investigate. She chatted amiably with a customer and banged out an espresso as Jacoby found the Voice Memo with the pizzaioli from Naples. Something about their conversation had Jacoby curious, and he was anxious to find out what it was, if anything at all.

Nicoletta returned, blew the bangs off her forehead and had a seat. Jacoby put the phone on the tabletop, cranked up the volume, and activated the recording. Nicoletta smiled at the sound of familiar dialect and listened intently, nodding, pulling at the corners of her mouth. She let out a quick laugh and then blushed. And then her face went serious.

"What?" Jacoby asked. "Che cos'è?"

Pinpricks across his hairline confirmed his suspicion that there was something to be learned from the recording. Nicoletta took a big breath and let it out. "Chi sono questi uomini?" she asked who the men were.

"Pizzaioli," Jacoby answered. "A Napoli."

"Pensano che voi siete..." she said and stopped when Jacoby held up a hand, knowing that the men thought of him and Bill as lovers.

Nicoletta blushed and said, "Buffo."

"Sì," Jacoby agreed, practicing patience, that it was funny, but he wanted to know more. "Ma, c'è piu. No?"

"Sì," Nicoletta confirmed and turned her head toward the barroom.

Jacoby put a hand on her forearm and begged her to finish the translation because he had to know. "Per favore," he said. "Devo sapere."

"Allora," she said. "Parlano di un'altro uomo. Forse l'ex fidanzato di Bill. Filippo. No?"

"Sì!" Jacoby confirmed the name of Bill's former lover. "Che c'è? Che c'è?"

Nicoletta turtled her head and looked into Jacoby's eyes. She spoke slowly and said, "Hanno detto che lui era lì recente e che sembrava molto triste."

Someone from the barroom called for the "Signorina" and Nicoletta rubbed Jacoby's forearm and left. He sat still and thought of what he had just learned: The rumors in Rome were true. Filippo was alive. He had just been in Naples for pizza.

Chapter 31

Jacoby walked in a trance out of the bar and into the sunlight of the piazza. He angled directly to the hotel, went inside and locked the door. He sat at the workstation near the counter. He picked up the house phone and put it down. He picked up the house phone again and dialed Bill's number. When the connection commenced, Jacoby hung up. So many thoughts raced through his head: The pizzaioli could have been mistaken; Dermot and the expats in Rome were just being silly. Why expose Bill to such trauma if they were all wrong? And why expose Bill to such trauma if they were correct? Why would Filippo be hiding from him anyway? Why would he be hiding at all? That part seemed too fantastic, yet it somehow made sense, not in a logical way but with a feeling Jacoby had had all along: the feeling of something lurking just out of sight.

Jacoby went to Giovanni's shoemaking shop and asked for a ride to the train station in Florence. On the way to the station, Jacoby shared, as best as he could, the story of the expats in Rome subscribing to a theory of Filippo being alive, corroborated, sort of, by the pizzaioli in Naples. Nicoletta had phoned Giovanni, as soon as Jacoby left the bar, to tell him of the translation's meaning, so he had some context to the story which made the conversation surprisingly successful. Amid all the excitement, Jacoby recognized that his Italian was improving, and his requests for Giovanni to stay in the barn and take care of Boy while he was away appeared perfectly understood. Giovanni nodded vigorously and tapped the small steering wheel with his thick fist.

The station was active after lunch on a weekday. Jacoby bought his Business Class ticket and fidgeted on the platform as pigeons fluttered around in the filtered light. He struggled sticking to one thought, and his head spun with the disparate narratives and the difficulties in having to address any of them. He did know that Bill needed to know, though how to even broach that evaded him. Little pings of anxiety rose from his sternum, and Jacoby practiced his breathing, in and out, slow and steady, in order to avoid the prompting of a panic attack. The gravity was inescapable and couldn't be willed away through logical thinking or denial. Jacoby wanted to call Helen, to talk it over and access her pragmatism, but she was surely in the museum, so he texted her a long message about everything that was happening. The train pulled into the station just as the message was being sent.

The car was mostly empty, and Jacoby stretched out in a corner section designed for four passengers, complete with a tabletop on which he tapped his fingers as the train hissed and squeaked and lurched its way out of the station and into the light. He called Bill.

"Pronto," Bill answered with exuberance.

"Hi, Bill," Jacoby said. "It's me."

"Jacoby," Bill sang. "I was just ready to call you."

"Why?" Jacoby asked, his head spinning with possibilities.

"To share the good news. We are officially in business as partners in the Hotel Floria-Zanobini."

"Oh, wow," Jacoby said, feeling relief. "That is great news."

"I couldn't agree more," Bill added. "And this trip to Rome has proven to be well worth it."

"I'll say," Jacoby quipped and then pivoted. "More good news is that I'm on my way back down, so we can celebrate tonight."

"Why in heaven would you be returning to Rome?" Bill asked, incredulous but still effusive.

"I need my suitcase," Jacoby lied. "Helen and I are going to take a trip once the festival is over."

"Oh," Bill sighed. "I intended on bringing it back with me, in what would have been a matter of days at this point."

"No worries," Jacoby said. "And this way we can celebrate together in Rome."

"Well, that is true," Bill said. "And I've got just the restaurant picked out."

.   .   .

It was midafternoon when Jacoby arrived in Rome, and he decided to walk from the train station to Campo de' Fiori since he had no bags and still needed time to think. He was also, and he knew it, in delay mode. Something was happening, but he didn't know what it was. He sensed a collision of sorts, yet this made him question his ability to reason. The unknown was driving him mad. He hoped, at least, to have a plan in place before telling Bill, but there didn't seem to be any playbook for telling a man that his dead lover might be alive or any way to predict how one would react.

The Roman sunshine soothed him some as he curved down the wide boulevard that fed into the city center. The city was calm, and shops were opening after riposo. He felt Rome's charm and sensed, in a small way, that the city was now part of him. He also recognized how such an efficient intimacy can be attained in Italy, how one can bond with a place so thoroughly in so little time. And that's what it was: time. Yes, there was, of course, boundless beauty, but time was the key factor - the pace of Italy permitted one to exist in a way that allowed life to be lived in little, steady celebrations that, through the continuity, generated an immense sense of well-being.

Jacoby took an espresso at a bar across from Piazza Venezia and stared in wonder at the whiteness and enormity of the 'Wedding Cake' building. Confident in his sense of direction, Jacoby avoided the avenue busy with vehicles and walked the shaded, narrow lanes among the ivy and serenity. He breathed in the colorful flowers nearing the end of their season. He passed the Pantheon and wandered down unfamiliar paths, blessedly lost. Within the resiny scent of the river, he rested on a sun-cloaked staircase and felt the warmth absorbed by his face spread through his body. He'd tell Bill after dinner. And now he'd have a gelato.

Under the tree-shaded parapet along the river, Jacoby walked past Castel Sant'Angelo and wondered how many days ago it was that he had visited on his excursions curated by Bill. He knew it was around a week, but the experience felt further in the past and, therefore, more familiar. Those were magical days, wandering Rome at Bill's behest, getting to know a city like one might a long, lost relative. Jacoby took pride in that he had enjoyed those days for what they were, and he recognized them as halcyon days before the conflict with the hunters and the rumors about Filippo. He thought of Filippo as he sat in the shade at a small, iron table in front of Gelateria del Teatro with the alternating flavors of pistacchio and stracciatella pleasing his palate and coating his tongue. The trees across the street and above the river swayed in dappled sunlight, and Jacoby wondered if the mysterious feeling he had was from the force of family lineage: Filippo, after all, was his mother's uncle. Sure, he'd never met the man or even knew he existed until arriving in Italy the previous spring, and even though Filippo and Bill had a love that lasted many decades, they were not of the same blood. They were not family in the ancestral sense, and maybe that was why this feeling was exclusive to Jacoby.

Jacoby entertained this fantastic idea and decided on its absurdity as he pieced together paths away from the river and toward the city center, where his dear friend would be waiting for him under an awning in front of a cafe on the edge of Campo de' Fiori. They would take an aperitivo before cleaning up for what was certain to be a spectacular dinner and an eventful evening.

Chapter 32

Bill was spry. Relieved and empowered as he was by the act of successfully navigating Italian bureaucracy, Jacoby had to hustle to keep up with him as they, both sharply dressed, left the apartment, said hello to Mama making pasta in the window of the restaurant next door, and crossed shifted cobblestones in the high afternoon light to Corso Vittoria Emanuele II.

They hailed a taxi, and the car followed a route along the river, past Castel Sant'Angelo and toward Vatican City. Bill informed Jacoby of their plans for the evening, which involved two of his favorite Roman treasures: The Galleria Borghese and Spazio Niko Romito. Bill had decided prior to their arrival in Rome that neither treasure would be visited until the mission was met, and this was why Jacoby had been encouraged to find the museum, on an earlier excursion, but to not go inside. The story of the restaurant's significance would be shared over dinner.

Bill stared out the window with contentment as the car rolled into the lush greenspace of Villa Borghese among the umbrella pines and manmade ponds among the lush grounds. Romans and tourist groups walked and biked and rested on benches. The evening was cool, and Jacoby lowered his window to take in the sweet air of the natural surroundings. The museum required a reservation, and Bill had made the arrangements. They were also timed to arrive just before 5:00 to slip in ahead of the cutoff to an uncrowded museum. The taxi warbled over stones up to the entrance, and Jacoby marveled at the stunning off-white villa, itself a work of art framed by a billowing treeline beyond and a crisp blue sky above.

People were leaving, and there was no line to enter. The cool halls were extravagant and still. Jacoby tried his best to match Bill's enthusiasm, though he was burdened by his friend's potential reaction to the looming revelation. It was precisely the wrong mood to be in for a museum visit, which required patience and perseverance along with an eye open to beauty, but Jacoby followed along beside Bill, listening to his whispered wealth of knowledge. Bill had provided tours of the museum to students from the university, and even some tourists, and he, very much like Helen, had the right touch when it came to what to share and how much. Still, Jacoby had to feign interest and enthusiasm, especially in the collection of paintings which were lovely in color and detail but somewhat dull in subject. Portraits bored him, though at least there was some diversity here with regard to gender and status. There was also, much to his delight, not an abundance of baby Jesus paintings.

The sculptures were far more interesting, and Bill dedicated a lot of praise to the genius of Bernini. It was hard to deny the magnificence of his work, and Jacoby decided - also recognizing how moved he was by the "Veiled Christ" work in Naples - that sculpture was his visual art preference. The works, often in actual size or even in grand scale, on display throughout the city, not just in museums but often in public spaces, validated the best of human artistic capability. Bill placed Jacoby in the perfect position to appreciate "Apollo and Daphne." He lost track of time taking in the details of the stunning statue while simultaneously wondering how a living person could create something so beautiful yet accessible to the average eye. It was the intention, after all, to create beauty for everyone to appreciate that Jacoby admired most in art and in life. And he kept this idea of good intentions with him as they toured the rest of the limited collection as the time for dinner approached.

·   ·   ·

Jacoby and Bill walked out of the museum as darkness settled over the gardens. They exited the grounds from under a canopy of umbrella pines onto an avenue humming with the last throes of daylight. The quartiere was quiet, and Bill explained, with only minor interruption from passing cars and motorini, that the restaurant was relatively new to Rome, just established before he and Filippo had moved to Florence five year prior, but it was an outpost of arguably the best restaurant in Italy: Ristorante Reale in the region of Abruzzo.

Bill and Filippo would go to the restaurant in Abruzzo twice a year and stay at the boutique hotel in which it was located. The property itself was masterfully converted from an abbey and on lush grounds outside a quaint town nestled in the hills. There was also a gourmet cooking school on the premises, adding an ambiance of young people learning an ancient art. Bill claimed that it was his favorite place on earth, elegant and serene, owned and operated by masters of hospitality and a chef of the highest stature.

"And who would that be?" Jacoby asked as they navigated Piazza Verdi as car lights came on.

"Why, him," Bill said, stopping in front of a modernist door marked, within a mirrored frame, by raised words in metal.

"Spazio" Jacoby said, a playful tone in his response.

"Below that," Bill said, playing along.

"Niko Romito," Jacoby said. "Cool name."

"Indeed," Bill agreed. "And his food is even better than his name."

Bill pulled open the heavy door, and they entered into a muted, cool foyer adorned with many plants among sleek, dark decor. A hum emanated from the interior, and the scents suggested a menu of diverse offerings. The dominant aroma came from a fryer, arousing Jacoby's appetite. Bill rubbed his hands and greeted the angular, lovely woman, dressed in business casual men's attire with a dress shirt and jacket but no tie, who approached smiling confidently beneath her stylish, short haircut. She seemed to match the room in chic elegance. Bill addressed her in Italian, cordially and with great warmth, and the woman responded in kind. They followed her through a neo-hipster barroom busy with young people taking small plates and aperitivi.

The back dining room had soft lights and muted colors, antique tables and chairs of wood spaced comfortably on parquet floors of shaded mahogany. The ceiling had wood beams and thatched bamboo threaded with ivy. Plants were everywhere, their green contrasting the dark design. Jacoby and Bill sat at a table for two in the corner beside a wall of glass that looked over a garden strung with exposed bulbs.

Bill looked content and whimsical. He laced his fingers and dropped his hands on the tabletop, his eyes following a young server, dressed in black slacks and a white oxford, who approached efficiently through the room half full of patrons. "Buonasera," she said accompanied by a dimpled smile and a tilt of her raven-haired head.

"Buonasera," both men said back in concert.

"Would you like the sparkling water or the flat?" she asked carefully in an adorable accent, full of lilt and inclusion of articles and vowels that wouldn't be there in native English.

"You're learning English," Bill acknowledged.

"Yes," she responded with a small blush. "I come to Roma from the Casa Donna in Abruzzo, where there is also the Ristorante Reale. To work here, I must speak English. It is OK, my English?"

"Yes, your English is wonderful," Bill said kindly. "And I know both the restaurant and the hotel very well."

"Oh, good. And thank you," she said with a small curtsy and a relieved giggle.

"I have an idea," Bill said. "My friend here is working on his Italian, so why don't we have him speak to you in Italian, and you can address him in English. My lips will be sealed."

"OK," she said with a playful shrug and in a way that even made that simple word charming.

"You want me to do all the ordering?" Jacoby asked Bill.

"I do," he said with a nod and sat back with his arms across his chest.

Jacoby shrugged in acceptance and smiled at the young woman when she turned her big eyes on him. "Primo," he said and then asked her name. "Come ti chiami?"

"Ah," she said. "My name is Rosanna. And you?"

"Io sono Jacoby," he said. "E questo è il mio amico Bill."

"A pleasure to meet you both," Rosanna said with a warmth inherent in Italian women.

"Grazie," Jacoby said confidently and then got to business. "Allora. Due martini, molto secco."

Rosanna nodded. "Two martini. Very dry," she said.

"Esatto," Jacoby responded.

"Very good," she said. "Thank you."

"Prego," Jacoby said.

"Martinis, eh?" Bill said to Jacoby once they were alone. "This could turn out to be quite an evening."

Jacoby nodded knowingly but kept the enormity of that potential to himself.

Chapter 33

"Do you recognize Rosanna from the hotel in Abruzzo?" Jacoby asked Bill while they waited on their martinis.

"Heavens no," Bill said. "She's far too young. The last time I was there, she was probably in secondary school."

"Right," Jacoby said. "Tell me more about the property. I might have to go with Helen."

Bill straightened in his chair and began a lovingly detailed description, which did sound like heaven, from the exquisite renovation of the former abbey right on down to the flatware. And, of course, there was the food, which came in multiple courses, beautifully presented, in a fashion made for tasting, accompanied by many supplements as compliments of the chef. Bill was describing a technique Chef Romito had invented where the water is extracted from something, like a piece of fruit, leaving only the essence of the flavor. This had Jacoby's palate very curious, and he was sold on Bill's description of the entire experience and he was, by the time their very dry martinis arrived in frosted glasses, committed to going to the piece of heaven in Abruzzo with Helen as soon as next week.

The men toasted each other and sipped the ice cold vodka. Bill's eyes went wide at the strength of the alcohol, and Jacoby thought he was clever to get Bill tipsy before telling him about Filippo. Of course, he'd have to make sure he was properly fed, as well, so Jacoby perused the menu and recognized it as being far more casual than the fare Bill had described at Ristorante Reale. He also recognized many of Bill's favorite dishes, which just happened to be among his own favorites as well.

"Are you ready to make the order?" Rosanna asked.

"Sì. Sono pronto," Jacoby confirmed. "Primo, un piatto di tonno sott'olio; poi, un piatto di polpo e patate; e finalmente, il pollo fritto, ovviamente."

Rosanna nodded in a pleased fashion and confirmed the order verbatim in English: "One plate of the tuna under oil; one plate of the octopus with potato; and, finally, the fried chicken, of course."

"Brava," Jacoby said.

"And to drink with the dinner?" she asked. "Maybe some wine?"

"Sì. Sì," Jacoby said quickly, having forgotten to pick a wine. He grabbed the wine list and put it down just as quickly. "Hai uno Pecorino di Abruzzo?"

"Yes, of course," Rosanna said, beaming, recognizing a coveted wine from her region.

"Scegli una bottiglia per noi," he asked her to choose a bottle for them.

"OK," she said, smiled, and left.

"Very good," Bill declared. "I do believe we are making progress."

He held up his martini glass, which was almost empty, in salute to Jacoby and then polished it off. "Shall we have another while waiting?"

•   •   •

Bill was boozy by the time the food arrived, his alcohol-infused enthusiasm evident in his raised voice, flushed face, and steady chatter. His subjects bounced around but were mostly related to the level of relief he felt about the hotel in Antella officially being theirs. For Bill, this was a long-denied status of a secure existence in Italy. For both of them, it was a fast road to citizenship, which had Jacoby uplifted too, and lifting his glass almost as often as his business partner and best friend, though the younger of the two clearly had a higher tolerance for hard alcohol. The other matter, one with far more import,

Jacoby knew would be best broached well after dinner, either at home or very close by. For now, he would focus on the food and company.

The tuna fillet that marinaded under oil for months was opaque in color but rich with the flavor of the fish and the aromatics that had surrounded it while encased. Jacoby identified the specific herbs and lemon enhancing the taste of tuna, washed it down with the round and crisp white wine, and did it all over again. "Hey," he said to Bill, apropos of nothing. "I'm going to write a memoir about living in Italy: Eat. Drink. Repeat. Get it?"

Bill nodded while forking in some of the tender white beans that the tuna was bedded upon. "Very good," he said while covering his full mouth.

Rosanna arrived with the plate of grilled octopus and potatoes along with clean plates and utensils for the new course. The dining area was full, and the atmosphere grew festive. Rosanna refilled their wine glasses and returned the bottle of Pecorino to a bucket of ice beside the table. "Everything OK?" she asked.

"Sì," Jacoby said and added another of his favorite expressions that was the gospel truth at the moment. "Tutto a posto."

Everything was in place as they tucked into the charred outer flesh of the firm octopus tentacles. "Oh my," Bill moaned, his face informed by rapture.

"I know," Jacoby agreed, after swallowing his first bite and going back for more. After that bite, he caught Rosanna's attention across the room and indicated they needed another plate of the polpo e patate.

"Excellent idea," Bill concurred as he spooned some crispy potatoes onto his plate, one of which he circled in the octopus juice and took in his mouth and moaned some more.

Both men made sounds of pleasure as they ate, a perfectly clear conversation that continued with the arrival of the second plate of the previous dish. What made this offering so incredible, Jacoby thought while eating, was that the flavors and textures and perfect preparation didn't lose any sense of enjoyment with each subsequent bite. One of the reasons Jacoby preferred to share plates is that the law of diminishing returns can set in, even with amazing food, after a certain amount of bites. Not here. He entertained the idea of ordering yet another plate but thought better of it. He did, though, ask for another bottle of the same wine.

"I have a wonderful idea," Bill said as they sat back to savor the lingering flavors of the polpo e patate while waiting for their fried chicken. "Let's walk all the way home to work off some of this food."

"Great idea," Jacoby agreed.

Bill sat up. "Better yet," he said with tipsy aplomb. "And we shall take a grappa on the roof of the Hotel Minerve to conclude our digestion over some of the best views in all of Rome."

"Works for me," Jacoby said as Rosanna approached with plates and cutlery, followed by a male helper ferrying a whole fried chicken on a platter surrounded by roasted potatoes.

"Good lord," Bill said. "This might call for multiple grappas at Minerve."

"Maybe," Jacoby said, thinking that on the roof of the hotel, accompanied by grappa and amazing view, would be the time to tell Bill about Filippo.

Chapter 34

They walked home in serious moonlight. Round and white as a porcelain plate, the lunar moon hung high and bright above the ancient Italian capital, blotting the stars and casting a veil of clear light over the city. The temperature had dropped, and the cool air kept Jacoby and Bill alert as they made their way alongside the Borghese greenspace. They were both full of alcohol but also stuffed with enough food to avoid inebriation.

Jacoby realized he had made a mistake in ordering when the fried chicken arrived, a portion dedicated to two people accompanied by what would be even more potatoes after the two rounds of polpo e patate. The mistake ended up being a blessing as they picked their way through much of the delicious chicken, brined and seasoned and lightly fried, and even some of the potatoes which were distinct from those previously served and served, themselves, as a nice absorber of alcohol. Still, they were feeling the booze.

Bill rambled on as they walked the first lengths and then grew quiet as they approached the Spanish Steps, the sound of their own steps clacking the cobblestones cloaked in light. It was a weeknight in autumn, and the streets were hushed a few hours before midnight. The commercial boulevards were nearly empty and the shops all shuttered. A few vehicles whizzed by, providing occasional sound in the otherwise silent night. They stopped on occasion at small fountains to take water, which Bill would also rub on his face and neck.

"We're almost there," Bill repeated with every turn on their path, referring to their destination of the Hotel Minerve which was near the Pantheon and still, Jacoby recognized from his previous walks, a good distance away. Bill was an avid walker, and Jacoby embraced the length they needed to travel as an opportunity to digest and sober up slightly before the news he had to share with Bill. As close as they had become, Jacoby had no idea how his friend would react. He couldn't even imagine his own reaction to such a startling report, though he needed to get it out there.

"We almost there?" Jacoby kidded as they turned another corner down a silent, dark lane.

"Very much so," Bill said. "I can practically taste the grappa."

After a few more turns, they were upon the Pantheon, its column illuminated but its doors closed. There were groups of young people around the fountain in the piazza and some unfortunate souls sleeping in the shadows. Jacoby and Bill passed through without notice and walked the wide lane toward the small Piazza della Minerve marked, appropriately enough, by Bernini's Elephant and Obelisk statue adjacent to a stately church and a grand hotel of faint pastel aglow in lights around the entrance and along each buttress of the floors above.

· · ·

The doorman held open the door, and Jacoby and Bill passed through an oak-framed entrance into an elegant lobby with marble floors and an elaborate ceiling of stained glass. Bill directed them to the elevator banks, and they were quickly delivered to the roof deck, where a bartender in a tuxedo greeted them cordially with a nod.

"Due grappe," Bill said, leaning into the bar but not taking one of the empty stools.

Jacoby wandered the nearly empty terrace and settled on a side far away from the small groups gathered at tables. The roofline of Rome spread out in spectacular fashion among domes and spires under the high and shiny moon. He could feel the cool in his lungs as he breathed deep and rehearsed his imminent conversation. Bill crossed the terrace slowly with a glass of grappa in each hand. He handed one to Jacoby and raised his own in salute. "To yet another wonderful day together," Bill said sweetly, and Jacoby's heart nearly broke.

"I have to tell you something," he said.

Bill pulled the glass from his lips before taking a sip. "What is it?" he asked. "Are you ill?"

Jacoby didn't want Bill to worry, so he got right to it. "Your friends in Rome think Filippo is alive." The words felt odd coming out of his mouth, almost as if they were spoken by somebody else.

Bill smiled. "Oh, I know," he said with a fey waive of his hand.

"You do?" Jacoby asked, feeling confused and foolish.

"Yes," Bill confirmed. "Dermot got drunk one night while you were back in Florence and told me the whole damn thing."

"And you didn't believe him?" Jacoby asked.

"Of course not," Bill said, somewhat annoyed. "It's preposterous."

"I dunno," Jacoby said gently. "Maybe there's something to it?"

Bill's face flushed and he looked over the roofline for a moment before turning hot eyes on Jacoby. "You should know better than to believe a bunch of old fags," he said bitterly. "Why on earth would Filippo be alive and hide such a fact from me?"

"I know it sounds crazy," Jacoby said. "I thought the same thing, but..."

"But what?" Bill interrupted. "God damn it."

Bill's uncharacteristic anger took Jacoby aback. "The pizzaioli," he mumbled.

"What?" Bill barked. "Have you lost your mind, boy?"

Bill's eyes were wide and his face ruddy. Jacoby reached for his phone and tried to explain. "In Naples, the pizzaioli, while you were in the bathroom, were talking about Filippo being there alone and not long ago."

"And you, the Italian expert, were able to translate that?" Bill asked, incredulous and snarky. "In dialect, no less."

"No," Jacoby said, holding up his phone. "I recorded it, and Nicoletta translated. She told me exactly what they said. I'll play it for you."

Bill held up his hand and looked away. "Nicoletta?" he said quietly and pulled at his beard. He turned back to Jacoby, perplexed for a moment, and then angry. He raised his glass of grappa and threw the contents in Jacoby's face.

The liquor burned Jacoby's eyes and filled his nose. He yanked up his shirt and forced the cotton into his clenched lids. The immediacy of the smell made him feel sick to his stomach, as did the reality of what had happened. By the time Jacoby was able to see clearly, Bill had gone. People were looking at him from across the terrace, and it felt as if the whole city had been witness to his humiliation.

He walked back across the terrace and got into the elevator without looking at anyone, though he felt the eyes upon him. He was wearing a glass of grappa on his shirt and face. Thankfully, the elevator was empty and the lobby quiet. He entered the night, feeling the cool on his wet shirt. Jacoby decided to leave Bill alone until morning.

Chapter 35

Jacoby walked to the Pantheon and used the fountain in the piazza to wash the sticky liquor off his face and neck. He even had to endure the unfortunate experience of intentionally filling his nose with water to rinse the smell of grappa that turned his stomach. It helped a little, but his shirt still wreaked. A headache, from booze and disappointment, crept in, and he felt very lost and a little scared. The moon had gone down, and the night was cold and dark. He walked out of the piazza and called Helen.

She picked up instantly and listened intently to the details of Jacoby's very long day, which had begun simply enough and now had him wandering around Rome in the middle of the night with a grappa-soaked shirt and nowhere to sleep.

"Check into a hotel!" Helen insisted. "You imbecile."

"I can't without a passport," Jacoby told her, having already thought through that scenario.

"Oh, right," she sighed with contrition. "Well then, go to the station and take a train home to Florence. You can sleep here, with me."

"That would be nice," Jacoby agreed, "but I feel like I should be here for Bill in the morning."

"Probably so," Helen said. "How about taking me for a walk around Rome? You can use your FaceTime."

Jacoby liked that idea, and he hung up, called Helen back using FaceTime and held up his phone to show her the streets that he walked, narrating the best he could. They kept up a steady conversation, and Jacoby was bolstered by her company and support. In some ways, this was more romantic than being in person as Helen, interrupted in the middle of the night, demonstrated a type of commitment to Jacoby that he had never known. The selfless act was not lost on Jacoby, and he consciously portrayed good spirits so as not to cause Helen concern.

"Hey," he said at one point, crossing a broad, uninteresting piazza lined with officious-looking buildings. "I discovered the kryptonite for Super Tuscan today."

"Oh, good lord," Helen mumbled playfully. "And just what is that?"

"Grappa in the face," Jacoby said. "Takes the powers right out of me."

"You really do need to drop that whole charade, you know?" Helen told him firmly but with silly pomp.

"Never!" Jacoby said, his voice echoing down an alley just entered.

They talked and laughed until the sound of falling water caught Jacoby's attention along with a glow at the end of the narrow path he walked. He picked up his pace, and the sound and glow increased until he turned the corner and faced the Fontana di Trevi in all its watery, sculpted splendor. Other than a young couple passionately kissing, Jacoby was all alone. He slowly navigated the immediate periphery of the pool, holding his phone for Helen to see.

"That was spectacular," Helen said after Jacoby returned to the quiet streets. "Now take me to the Spanish Steps. I want to see them at night and empty as well."

Jacoby led Helen on a bespoke, virtual tour of a silent Rome that lasted until his phone died in the wee small hours of the night. He was in a residential neighborhood with the crown of the Colosseum in the distance below. He walked in that direction, in search of familiar ground. The night quivered around him, and every random sound gave him a fright. Fatigue set in, and Jacoby operated on autopilot, following the path in front of him with very little thought beyond the desire for a warm bed and the need to carry on. His state felt trance-like.

Nearly at the bottom of the hill, around a quiet corner, lie a small piazza with a solitary figure under a street lamp, a man leaning against the wall, smoking a cigarette. Jacoby was not surprised as he smelled the smoke from blocks away and felt drawn in that direction. "Salve," the man said hello in a casual manner after Jacoby stopped short in clear view.

"Ciao," responded Jacoby. "Posso avere una sigaretta?"

The man waived him over, and Jacoby approached without trepidation. The man was dressed in layers of worn clothes, but he emitted no odor. As Jacoby drew closer, the man took off his thin, down jacket and handed it to Jacoby.

"Grazie," Jacoby said, putting on the jacket and feeling warmth emanate through his torso.

"You are welcome," the man said in a mostly neutral accent with hints of eastern Europe. Jacoby could see, now up close, that the man was pale with fair hair shaved tight to his scalp. His green eyes reflected in the lamp light. They were about the same age.

The man lit a cigarette off the one he already had and handed his pack and formidable lighter to Jacoby. They smoked in the silence, exhaling at the black sky. When they stepped on their finished butts, the man said, "Come," and walked across the piazza toward the Colosseum. Jacoby followed. After a few turns down silent alleys, the man stopped in front of a small door on a quiet block devoid of light. He looked both ways and then shouldered open the door. Jacoby ducked under the low archway and followed him into the darkness. It smelled of earth and rotting wood. Jacoby heard the flick of the lighter cap and the spark of the flame. The dingy room appeared, barren with a dirt floor and cracked walls, old furniture strewn around. Both men had to duck to avoid the wood-beamed ceiling as they crossed out of the main room and down a flight of creaky steps. Jacoby's heart beat hard though he was not afraid.

On the basement landing, the man turned to check on Jacoby, who nodded in return. They kept on through small compartments, among the musky squalor, to a hole in the ground with a wooden ladder. The man handed Jacoby his lighter and climbed down the ladder. Jacoby squatted next to the hole and extended the light. At the bottom, the man gestured for the lighter and encouraged Jacoby to join him. Jacoby flipped the lid of the lighter closed and was immediately immersed in darkness. "Here," the man said. Jacoby let the lighter go and heard it hit the ground. A moment later, the man's smiling face was illuminated. Jacoby, awash in relief, stepped carefully onto the ladder and climbed down.

They were in catacombs, with galleries in every direction. Some discarded religious ornaments were scattered on the ground, and one of the walls, the only one not of dirt, had a faded fresco. The man walked directly to a certain tunnel and proceeded without precaution, walking as fast as he could while hunched to avoid the ceiling. Jacoby followed, his teeth chattering and all of his senses fully engaged. Thoughts raced and images appeared, memories that felt personal but of no identifiable recollection. He also knew exactly where they were going.

After a few hundred yards, they came out of the tunnel into a small room with an iron ladder illuminated in slotted light. The man flicked closed his lighter and smiled at Jacoby. He climbed the ladder, pushed something aside and disappeared. Jacoby stared up at the empty hole backed only by darkness until the man's face poked out. "Come," he said.

Jacoby climbed the ladder, breathing the fresh air that dried the sweat on his neck. He pushed himself out of the hole onto the dusty surface and got to his feet. There was a metal grate beside the hole and natural light down a corridor that the man walked. Jacoby followed and gasped upon arrival in the open air. He had to steady himself as the impossibility of where he was reconciled with the fact that he knew their destination all along.

The Colosseum surrounded them, its rectangular windows of the upper facade gathering the faint light offered by the night sky. Arched entrances in tiers circled the amphitheater where they stood on a floor of grass and dirt and stone. It was truly a stadium, bigger than it appeared from the outside. The rush of history made it hard to breathe, and Jacoby did not move at first. He eventually turned very slowly in every direction and marveled at the achievement. Cats mewed among their feet, aggressively bumping into their shins and calves. "Come," the man said. "It's best to keep moving or be eaten alive by the beasts."

They scaled some wooden planks up to the first tier above the stadium floor and walked the circumference. The surreality of the experience made it hard to acknowledge the specifics, and the man did not speak at all as they walked. *Some tour guide*, Jacoby thought in a moment of lucidity before returning to his trance as he toured the Roman Colosseum in the middle of the night with a silent stranger. After a full turn, they scaled an incline of ruin and sat on a row of marble. Jacoby imagined the scene that might have played out in front of those who sat in this exclusive area, of the savage events on the ground among the roaring crowd of ancient Romans. He wondered how much blood had been spilled in the soil below. He suddenly felt very tired. His head bobbed and popped back up.

"Make a rest," the man said. "I will keep the cats away with my flame."

"You sure?" Jacoby asked.

"Yes," the man said. "I will wake you at the bruzzico."

"What's that?" Jacoby asked, aware of the word but not sure how.

"You will see," the man said, brandishing his lighter. "Now rest."

Chapter 36

Jacoby woke up outside of the Colosseum, on the grassy expanse near the ruins of the Forum. He sat upright under an umbrella pine, his back against the trunk. He assumed his adventure with the man in the catacombs and the Colosseum had all been a dream brought on by lack of sleep. Surely, he had blacked out as if drunk from exhaustion and safely settled where he was at some point very late in the night. The spectacular and vivid dream must have been the result of such extreme fatigue and also inspired by the vicinity to the Colosseum where he had settled for the night. Jacoby, more than anything else, felt relief to have made it through the long night safely, and he dozed intermittently as the light appeared in spots around Palatine Hill and a new day loomed for the Eternal City. The first true light of sunrise appeared along the cobalt blue horizon in a streak of orange, and Jacoby knew this was the bruzzico.

Stiff and cold, Jacoby rubbed the chill from his bones and walked the main road between the ruins as the last wisps of night wind shimmied the tree branches. The sun warmed him as the city came to life. Jacoby took a caffè and a cornetto at a bar near Piazza Venezia. He used the bathroom there and cleaned himself up as best he could. He felt grungy, covered in dust and soot and grappa, and the idea of a shower kept interrupting his thoughts about Bill as he walked the familiar route back to Campo de' Fiori.

The market was setting up for the day, and the bright colors of the fruits and vegetables bolstered Jacoby's mood. Before ringing the apartment's buzzer, Jacoby ducked into the hidden courtyard and walked to the fountain in its center. He did a full turn, carefully studying the buildings and the objects within. There was not the same sense of a presence he had detected before, but it occurred to him that nothing in the courtyard had changed: The bikes and balls and other inanimate objects were exactly where they had been all along. There was no sight of a person or sound from within the walls or the bright-colored doors that never opened. It felt, in some ways, like a movie set. A facade. He was tempted to knock on some doors, to see if anyone would answer or just to wait in the courtyard for someone to appear, but his thoughts went back to the priority of finding Bill and the hope of making things right.

The buzzer to the apartment went unanswered, but the door to the building was open, as was the door to the unit they occupied on the top floor. Bill was not there. Some of his things remained, but his travel bag was gone. A set of keys were on the small kitchen counter. Jacoby's belongings were where he left them, and he plugged his phone into a charger before taking a shower. When he returned towel-wrapped from the bathroom, his phone indicated a voicemail. Jacoby put the phone on speaker and activated the message from Bill:

My dear Jacoby. I'm terribly sorry about last night. I was overcome and reacted terribly. I do hope you will accept my apology. I'm sure it's difficult to imagine the range of emotions one feels in such a moment, but I do hope you will forgive me nonetheless. There was a pause filled by the sound of a deep breath. *The reality is that I harbored a similar notion of Filippo not being dead, though I kept it suppressed, assuming it was just a coping mechanism of some sort, but after our exchange last night I was overwhelmed with a thought - a thought that relates to our mutual appreciation of fate being a gift. I left the hotel and took a taxi to Spazio where Rosanna was thankfully still there. She described a man who visits regularly who does not go by the name of Filippo but sounds precisely like him. I've decided to go see for myself. I'm leaving early this morning on a bus for Abruzzo. There are keys on the kitchen counter for you. I have my own set. I assume you will go back to Antella for the festival. Please lock up and hold the keys for me. I will call you as soon as I have anything to report. Sorry, again, to have wasted such lovely grappa.* Bill chuckled and ended the call with *Ta*.

Jacoby sat on the bed and chuckled as well. It was pretty funny, in retrospect, that Bill had doused him in grappa, and he imagined that memory would come up often, but his thoughts quickly turned to the crux of Bill's message. Jacoby's head spun, and his lungs filled with a sense of magic at the deliverance of a latent feeling that had been lingering all along. The fantastic news, and the reconciliation with Bill, elated him and offered a tremendous sense of relief. Fatigue washed over Jacoby, like the waters of the grand fountains, and he fell back on the bed into a deep sleep on top of the covers without dreams of strangers who took him to forbidden places and taught him the meaning of new words.

•   •   •

Jacoby slept most of the morning and caught a train that arrived in mid-afternoon at Santa Maria Novella in Florence. He was tempted to go see Helen, but he simply texted her that he was home and safe, as an urgency to get back to Antella overrode his desires and directed him into the backseat of a taxi. As the car veered through the streets of Florence and onto the wide road that circled the city center, Jacoby prioritized finalizing transportation of the guests from Florence to the village as this was the last major matter to resolve. That and security. Agita rose through his sternum as the taxi warbled up the rock-studded road toward Paolo's villa. Jacoby stood in front of the gate as the driver executed a careful three-point turn and pointed the car back down the hill in a cloud that drifted over the valley. He reached around the fence and found the button on the box that triggered the fence. Relief and joy came to him as Boy bound down the drive between the barn and the villa, his ears flapping and his tail wagging.

Behind the barn, the grove was empty, the olive trees stripped of their fruit, their musk emanating from the detritus on the ground. Paolo was probably at the consortium, overseeing the pressing and bottling of his and others' bounty. The romance of the harvest excited Jacoby, and he was grateful for his role, even as complicated as it had become. He took Boy for a walk around the property, and they sat on the ridge overlooking the city of Florence in the burnished orange light of sunset that settled in the hills beyond the city and upon the towers and domes and palaces, the rooftops and bridges and shining river of the city itself. Jacoby hoped his beloved Florence would open his mind to ideas, but none came. And then his beloved from the city called.

"Pronto," Jacoby answered, knowing it was Helen but always eager to use the Italian phone greeting.

"I've got your transportation problem and your security problem settled in one fell swoop," Helen said, bypassing any greetings.

"I'm fine," Jacoby said formally. "And how are you?"

"Do you want to be cute or do you want to hear how I solved your problems?" Helen asked with her feisty and adorable impatience.

"OK," Jacoby caved. "You got me. What's up?"

"You'll have to come to Florence to find out," Helen said, her tone threaded with temptation. "And take me to dinner first and then to bed. And maybe, just maybe, if I'm properly satisfied, I'll let you know all that I have done for you."

Jacoby sighed and petted Boy's head which was in his lap. "I'm sorry," he said. "I just got back, and I can't leave Boy so soon. How about you come here?"

"Let me get this straight," Helen said with mock-seriousness. "You want me to come to you for dinner and sex and to present a gift, essentially, that I've arranged on your behalf?"

"The dinner will be really good," Jacoby teased. "With my best wine."

"I'll be there in an hour," Helen said. "Meet me in the piazza."

Chapter 37

Jacoby and Boy walked down the slope to the village, passing through the still olive groves, the gnarled branches naked of their fruit. Thin clouds stretched overhead, diminishing the sun. Jacoby smelled the season ready to turn, and he was both excited and apprehensive about all that would happen before the inevitable arrived with time. For now, though, he would enjoy the walk with his dog to the village he adored where he would shop for dinner and later meet his love in the piazza.

It was after the riposo, and the piazza was busy with shoppers and socializers in the long shadows. Village children played soccer. There was time before Helen's arrival, so Jacoby took a medium cup of gelato and enjoyed it while sitting on the precipice of the statue, among the old men in tweed caps who spoke of something Jacoby did not understand. As much as Jacoby wanted, needed, to improve his Italian, he did enjoy simply listening to Italians speak as their words without meaning were music. The chorus of old men sang a song that accompanied Jacoby's enjoyment of his regular gelato combination of pistacchio e stracciatella.

"Arrivederci," Jacoby said when finished. "Buona serata."

"Buona serata, Jake," some of them said and all of them acknowledged his departure with respective gestures as he walked off across the piazza.

At the butcher shop, Jacoby went in while Boy waited outside. Jacoby loved the aesthetic of Italian butcher shops, where the products were displayed like decorations, not groceries. There was no odor, other than some aromatics. Nothing was wrapped in plastic. Everything was of the highest quality. The meat glistened behind sparkling glass counters. Prosciutto legs and cylinders of cheese dangled from the ceiling. The products on the shelves were in glass containers, not cans. The butchers themselves were men of great respect, of civic stature, and the butcher of Antella was no exception: fair-haired and rosy cheeked, slightly stooped but still buoyant and bravo, energetic about his work. Lorenzo didn't speak much to Jacoby, but he was always welcomed warmly in the shop and treated with great deference. It was Lorenzo, a fourth generation butcher, who had provided Bill and Jacoby the information about Jacoby's ancestors from the village, the story of the heiress, Jacoby's grandmother, who had run off with the American soldier during World War II. And it was also Lorenzo who butchered the cinghiale Jacoby had killed, providing Bill with the prime meat for the ragu he made for the sagra and keeping the legs and other parts to himself, as payment, to be used in every imaginable way possible to ensure that the animal's life was not taken in vain.

"Vieni qua," Lorenzo instructed Jacoby to join him in the back of the shop.

The spacious room had tiled walls and a floor of checkerboard marble. The wooden butcher blocks were immaculate and adorned with instruments for butchering. There were all sorts of devices for cutting and grinding and sharpening. Huge sinks. A meat locker, with a small window in the door, had huge cuts hung from hooks. Jacoby appreciated the preferential treatment, and he made a point of visiting the butcher on a very regular basis. He also recognized the butcher as almost a sheriff-type figure, a man with a shotgun he was not afraid to fire, as he did to end the brawl at the village sagra. Jacoby was glad to have him on his side, and he was also glad to have Lorenzo catering the festival at the consortium, where he would serve porchetta with lots of sides.

"Tutto a posto per sabato?" Jacoby asked, confirming unnecessarily that the butcher would be ready for Saturday's event.

Lorenzo flattened his lips and nodded sanctimoniously. He directed Jacoby to a stainless steel table that held a massive carcass of pork. He motioned along the loin with his finger and then dug that finger into his puffy cheek. Jacoby understood the translation: That huge loin would be separated from the carcass, trimmed expertly, butterflied, stuffed with seasonings and aromatics, rolled, sealed in pork skin that would be scored and roasted into the gastronomic ecstasy known as porchetta to be sliced thin and devoured by the guests of the festival. Jacoby could not wait. And he amused himself by thinking that no matter how things went at the festival, there would be porchetta. It also gave Jacoby an idea for dinner.

"Posso avere una cotoletta di maiale?" he asked for a pork cutlet.

Lorenzo flattened his lips and nodded with approval. He went to the front of the shop and came back with a pork loin on the bone, which he used a hand saw to separate from a two-inch chop. The chop was pounded with the flat side of a heavy clever, wrapped in butcher's paper and presented to Jacoby as a gift along with some scraps for the dog.

"Grazie," Jacoby said.

"Prego," Lorenzo said and then went back to work.

"Ci vediamo sabato," Jacoby said his farewell and walked out of the back room, through the storefront and into the fading daylight where Helen, under a felt fedora, with her back to the shop, sat on the small curb petting Boy. A hand to his chest covered Jacoby's walloping heart.

.   .   .

The frutta e verdura stand on the near corner of the piazza was owned by two miserable sisters who did not, at least from Jacoby's experiences, speak to each other. Both in house dresses, they sat, respectively, behind the counter and in the entryway to the storage area in back. The vibe of the shop saddened Jacoby, in such contrast to the vibrant fruits and vegetables that filled the crates under the awning up front and almost the entirety of the floor space within. Jacoby imagined they had a fight at some point, probably many years ago. He also recognized, despite their age, they had many years to live as elderly Italians were as formidable, physically, as they came.

The sisters seemed to like Jacoby or at least took some enjoyment in his strange presence among the villagers. He took a handful of arugula in a brown paper bag along with a sack of robust tomatoes that the sister at the counter told him had come up from Calabria. As she weighed the selections, Jacoby, in careful Italian, invited her and her sister to the festival on Saturday. She registered the invitation and then shook a swollen hand in front of her ample bosom at the impossibility of such an offer. Jacoby took it in stride and met Helen and Boy outside.

They walked up the hill in the staticky light of dusk's final moments. The colors in the sky reflected off the streaks of clouds. Jacoby held the dinner sacks to his chest with one hand and Helen's hand in the other as they strode together at a brisk clip: Jacoby having made this walk many times and Helen who essentially walked for a living. Boy kept a few paces ahead, checking back frequently on his people. On occasion, he'd dash into the growth after a smaller animal.

They reached the ridge road as darkness prevailed, and they walked carefully on the path beside the two-lane road as car lights flashed occasionally past. They were soon upon the track to the villa, and lightning bugs surrounded them among the fervent last efforts of insects to extract anything useful from the curtains of herbs and growth that dangled from the Etruscan wall opposite the valley that hoarded darkness in its belly and smelled of flowers.

The lights to the villa were on, and they were through the gate and up the ramp to the barn before the autumn chill settled. It felt so good, to Jacoby, to do something as simple as coming home with his girlfriend and his dog and sacks of delectable groceries for dinner. Before entering the barn, he grabbed a fistful of sage from the hedge alongside the terrace. Inside, he fed Boy the scraps mashed in with his house-made kibble, and then prepped the kitchen for making dinner. Helen connected to the Wi-Fi, put on an Otis Redding album, and went to the credenza to fix drinks.

"You have whiskey!" she declared. "And bitters!"

"I love an occasional Manhattan," Jacoby said.

Helen nodded in approval. "Perfect for a chilly night," she said.

While Helen worked on the cocktails, Jacoby made a workstation on the kitchen counter with respective bowls of egg wash and bread crumbs. He unwrapped the pork cutlets and seasoned each thoroughly with salt and pepper before dredging them in the egg wash then pressing them in the breadcrumbs, making sure each side had a thorough crust.

"Which wine should I open?" Helen asked from the credenza once the cocktails were prepared.

"How about the one from Volpaia," he answered.

"Brilliant idea," she said and pulled the bottle of Chianti Classico Riserva they had procured during the last trip to Chianti country and the tiny village of Volpaia. She popped the cork and left it to breath on the credenza. She brought the cocktails over to the kitchen counter and handed one to Jacoby. They chinked glasses and sipped the complex drink, full of competing flavors dominated by the pungent, oaky rye.

Jacoby put the massive frying pan that came with the barn on the larger of the two burners of his tiny oven's stovetop. From the fridge, he took a knob of butter he kept for special occasions and dropped it in the pan. As it began to melt, Jacoby swirled in a generous amount of olive oil and waited for the foam of the butter to subside. When it had, and the lipids had mixed and heated, he added the cutlets. They sizzled perfectly, indicating the perfect heat to seal and fry but not burn. Helen began setting the table beside the credenza and poured two balloon glasses with ruby wine. It was dark outside the windows, but their little space was full of light and aromas and music. And two very happy people. Boy rested on his haunches on the tile floor, watching the humans do the dance of dinner preparation, privy to their joy and the comfort it exuded.

With the first side of the cutlet properly sealed, Jacoby carefully turned each with a serving fork and allowed the second side to settle in the lipid before basting the top, using a simple spoon, with the excess butter and oil. On an oversized wooden cutting board set on the counter, Helen chopped the tomatoes and combined them with the arugula in a ceramic bowl. She added a pre-made vinaigrette from the fridge and tossed the salad. When the cutlets were done, a perfect camouflage pattern of beige and browns, Jacoby transferred them to the cutting board to be seasoned with salt and anointed with a squeeze of lemon. He quickly fried the sage in the pan drippings and put them over the cutlets as a most decadent garnish. The salad was piled alongside the meat. It all looked so perfect there on the platter that he changed his mind about bringing it to the small table beside the credenza.

"Let's just eat here," he suggested. "Fuck the plates."

"Fine with me," Helen agreed. "Fuck the plates. And the table, too."

She ferried over the wine and cutlery. They touched glasses and experienced a taste of aged wine from one of the world's most prestigious regions, about 20 km from where they stood, alongside a kitchen counter digging into a perfectly prepared pork cutlet, crusty on the outside and tender within, seasoned throughout and paired with a zesty salad of tomatoes and arugula. They moaned in tandem with the first bite.

Chapter 38

On the day before the festival, Jacoby was anxious. He hadn't heard from Bill since the voice message about going to Abruzzo to find Filippo. It was hard to keep those happenings from slipping into his thoughts, but he also had other concerns. Helen's plan for both transporting guests from Florence proper and providing security was beyond brilliant, and there was much relief about having those important matters potentially covered, though many other physical logistics, and an imposing personal one, remained, so he left the hotel after a few hours of work in the morning with the intention of spending the rest of the day on the estate.

A layer of low clouds covered the sky, and the air smelled of dead leaves as Jacoby motored through the forest-bordered roads outside of the village. The air cooled with his ascent, and it occurred to him, as he cleared the trees and entered the estate's vast, open property, that there was no contingency plan for rain. There had been no rain, of which he was aware, since he'd arrived in Tuscany the previous June, but he had heard much of the rainy season scheduled to commence at the end of autumn, and he hoped the cool temperature of the day and appearance of cloud cover were not the portentous sign of the rainy season's premature arrival.

A premature arrival, and a potentially portentous one, awaited Jacoby at the estate in the presence of Dolores, his personal logistic concern, who had arrived a day ahead of schedule. Her baby blue Alfa

Romeo Spider was parked on the lawn next to the villa, and her voice could be heard coming from within the recently renovated walls as soon as Jacoby cut the engine on the motorino. Jacoby adored Dolores, and he was happy that they maintained a relationship after the collapse of his engagement to her "Dear Cousin Claire." Their relationship, though, was now in large part professional, and Jacoby had some doubts about working for someone as privileged and demanding as Dolores.

Jacoby tried to discern her tone as he hurried inside, and relief washed over him as it became clear she was offering effusive praise to someone who was not afforded the opportunity to respond. Dolores' Italian fluency included familiarity with various dialects as she had traveled extensively over the entire peninsula before settling on Tuscany for the vacation home she visited often from her base in London. Jacoby hurried through the spacious, light-filled living room, which would serve as the villa's reception area, toward the voice in the kitchen.

"Hi, Dolores," Jacoby said as he entered the massive, sparkling, modern kitchen with a country motif highlighted by terracotta floors, whitewashed walls, and a wood-beamed ceiling.

The person to whom Dolores had been speaking was Bruna, who may have been overwhelmed by everything that was Dolores, this woman essentially from another planet than the one where Bruna had lived her long life in a subservient role defined by gender. The elderly woman smiled at Jacoby as if she'd been saved and made a praying gesture with her soft hands as Dolores walked away from her to greet Jacoby.

Dolores wore a satin, forest-green romper and white designer sneakers. Her hair had been tinted a luxurious blonde and her thick, tanned arms wiggled over her head that was tilted coquettishly to indicate her approval. "Oh, Jacoby," she said before wrapping her arms around him and pressing her formidable body against his lithe frame. "It's just spectacular."

"Thank you," he said, tucked into her softness and scent of Chanel. "Have you seen the whole villa?"

She separated suddenly and shook Jacoby's shoulders as her eyes widened. "I have, thanks to this charming woman - Bruna, is it? - and I could not be more pleased," she said earnestly before throwing on a naughty look. "And you know how hard I am to please."

Jacoby laughed, reminded of how much fun they had together when Dolores pursued her Master's degree at a fashion college in Manhattan. "Have you checked on the consortium?" he asked.

"No," she said with an officious tone. "You can accompany me there now."

She took Jacoby by the arm and led him through the grand villa and into the sunlight that had dispersed the cloud cover.

.　　.　　.

Down a slope 100 yards from the villa, the consortium was originally an abbey that predated the villa itself. The low-slung, modest complex was built of stone. It's main corridor had been gutted and repurposed with equipment for the production of wine and olive oil while the remaining branches of the building now provided an area for bottling and labeling with seasonal housing above in the cloisters for migrant workers who were busy all day within and around the facility. The wooden doors of arched-entryways to the production area were open, and within stainless steel vats, bushels of grapes were being fed. In another area, a medieval-looking device pressed olives into a green liquid that approached an emerald hue in its brilliance.

Dolores walked around the main production room as if she owned it, and she did. At least, she owned a part of it with Paolo and a group of his cronies who were nowhere to be found.

"And where are my partners?" she asked Jacoby.

Jacoby stopped Dolores' one-woman tour with a gentle hand inside her elbow. "Look, Dolores," he said carefully yet with resolve. "I can't be the intermediary between you and Paolo and company or be responsible for what's happening here."

"Really," she interrupted, putting her hand on a shifted hip. "You are receiving my payments, are you not? Because if you're not..."

Jacoby jumped in quickly, with a knowing smile and his hands up. "Yes, Dolores, I am receiving your payments, but those have to do with the work on the villa exclusively, and you seem to be happy with the results, correct?"

Dolores didn't answer. She turned to study the men - who had been stealing glances at the exchange between the two young, English-speaking strangers with distinct accents and body language that implied a conflict of sorts - looked away and focused on their work. When Dolores was done surveying the room, as if her glances were establishing dominion, she untucked her lips and nodded permission for Jacoby to continue.

"You asked me to help with the event, and as far as I can tell, I've done everything, which is fine, I guess because I'm happy to help you, always, but beyond that I've got no part in the consortium and the production."

"Have they been no help at all?" Dolores asked.

"They've been here, a lot," Jacoby said, eager to defend Paolo and the others from Dolores' wrath. "But they seem to think the festival event is entirely my responsibility."

"I wonder how they got that impression?" Dolores mused.

Jacoby made the 'Katie Holmes Face' that they employed as a drinking game device during Dolores' days in New York. Her mouth immediately formed an outraged 'O' and she smacked Jacoby playfully on the arm. "Don't make that face at me, you petulant cock-splatt!"

Jacoby cracked up, and Dolores tried not to join him before giving up and a contrite crossing of her arms over her great bosoms. "Fine," she said. "Maybe I mentioned to them that I'd oversee the festival. I couldn't possibly leave it to those men. There would probably only be a leg of prosciutto and a wheel of cheese."

"Yeah, probably," Jacoby was eager to agree and keep Dolores lighthearted.

She looked around the room again and acknowledged that things seemed to be in order and efficient. "They must be off to lunch," she said of her partners.

"Probably," Jacoby said again.

"Oh stop being so damn agreeable," Dolores insisted. "Let's have lunch at that lovely cantinetta where we celebrated our bounty from the auction. You can tell me all about the plans for tomorrow. Surely, Paolo and the lads will be back by the time we've returned."

Jacoby sure hoped so, for their sakes.

Chapter 39

Lunch with Dolores, which could have extended into dinner, lasted only a few hours. After a mixed-plate of antipasti, including some burrata and a crostini of tomatoes and white beans, they had plates of fresh tagliatelle buried - per Dolores' instruction - in a mountain of shaved white truffles procured from Piedmont, followed by enormous ribs roasted over open flames accompanied by crisp potatoes. They took a dessert plate of pear and fresh pecorino. Local wine was sipped throughout, and Dolores agreed with Jacoby that their Chianti was underrated, confirming her wise investment and putting her in good spirits throughout the lunch of which she insisted on paying.

Dolores was also pleased with the list of journalists and bloggers coming to the festival, many of whom she followed on Instagram. Jacoby was impressed by the plans Dolores had to increase productivity at the consortium through investment in updated equipment and more labor. He also adored the label she designed, featuring a sketched cinghiale, for both the wine and olive oil bottles. Her talents, in business and creativity, were easy to overlook because of her grandiosity, but Jacoby recognized what Dolores brought to her endeavors and was so grateful that she had purchased the estate that once belonged to his family since she, in a weird way, felt like family. They laughed a lot through lunch, and Dolores let Jacoby drive her incredible sports car back to the estate where he would make sure everything was in place for the next day as she sought out Paolo and the other partners for a conversation of which Jacoby would, thankfully, not be privy.

Jacoby handled his affairs at the estate and arrived home late in the afternoon. He took Boy for a long walk and made himself a simple dinner of chickpeas basking in warm olive oil with rosemary and garlic, mopped up with focaccia. He spoke by phone with Helen for a while after dinner, confirming the plans she had conceived and arranged for the media guests along with the most formidable security detail Jacoby could imagine. He truly did love her more for this effort not because it helped him so much but she bothered to think of it, on his behalf, in the first place. She also asked about Bill, and Jacoby was sad to have no answer. Helen encouraged him to call Bill, but Jacoby felt that would be inappropriate. He also felt, but kept to himself, that the silence from Bill indicated something was happening, buttressed by a similar sense that he had had in Rome and accompanied him through his seemingly uneventful day: That fate was, once again, about to be delivered.

. . .

The sun shined through the open doors of the Juliet balcony off Jacoby's room. He jumped from bed, feeling well-rested and invigorated. He would do his best to make the most of this day and deal with the consequences regardless. The idea was just to put this day behind them as it had consumed his thoughts and dictated his actions for so long. He wanted closure on this part of their new endeavor; and he wanted to take a small holiday with Helen. But mostly, though, he wanted to know what was happening with Bill. Jacoby checked his phone and had his first pang of annoyance at Bill's silence. Surely he knew that Jacoby waited anxiously for word, or even news of no news. Then Jacoby thought, with a dose of shame, of how overwhelming this must all be for Bill.

Jacoby showered and dressed and focused on his day. A major decision, and one he'd been avoiding, was whether or not to bring Boy. On the one hand, it would be cute and socially convenient to have a dog mingling among the guests at the festival and bounding round the property; on the other hand, if the hunter's showed up, they might manage to take back the dog again. Any consideration of the matter was eliminated by Boy sitting on his haunches at the barn's door, a look of pleading on his face and in his eyes as if he knew the risks and wanted desperately to come along. "OK, Boy," Jacoby sighed with relief of essentially having the decision made for him. "Let's go."

They waited outside the villa's gate, and soon Giovanni's Fiat bumped up the track trailed by billowing dust. "Ciao!" he yelled out his open window upon arrival and then carefully turned the car around. Jacoby and Boy got in the backseat and the dog lurched toward the passenger seat to be petted and fed by Nicoletta who had brought her surrogate pet a cornetto.

"Pronto?" Giovanni asked Jacoby while looking in the rearview mirror as the Fiat descended the access road pinched between the Estruscan wall draped in herbs and the plush valley sown with poppies.

"Sì," Jacoby said, with his eyes on the mighty Cypress trees that lined the ridge beyond the valley. The beauty of the surroundings distracted him from any anticipation, and Jacoby was reminded of those tortuous moments before a gig as a musician or a game as a high school athlete when the waiting nibbled at his nerves. He lowered the car window and breathed in the pine and rosemary, letting the nature of Italy soothe him, as it always did, yet somehow providing stimulus as well. "Sì," he said again and bumped his fist off Giovanni's headrest.

Giovanni and Nicoletta exchanged bemused looks and glanced back at Jacoby with curiosity. He smiled at his friends and touched both of their shoulders. Then he sat back and petted Boy as the Fiat joined the road toward Florence bordered by empty olive groves with the leaves of the trees shimmering green-grey in the lemon light. They wound down to the city and then cut back toward the village on wooded roads dappled in light that split the trees of birch and oak. When the trees parted, they were on the estate. Jacoby was the first one out of the car, followed soon by Boy, as if both knew it was going to be a monumental day.

Chapter 40

On a plateau down from the villa and fronting the consortium operations, migrant workers set up retractable tables and chairs under the direction of Bruna. Jacoby kissed both of her cheeks and hurried to the far reaches of the expanse to greet the butcher. He stood behind a long, wooden table sharpening a gigantic knife. The table, covered in checkered cloth, had an oblong centerpiece wrapped in foil and many smaller plates and bowls sealed with plastic. A figure behind the butcher was building a fire pit using bricks he unloaded from the back of their van parked on the grass nearby.

"Ohhh!" the butcher bellowed when Jacoby approached. "Come stai, Johnny?"

Jacoby smiled, as he always did upon the butcher's unique greeting. "Bene," he said. "E tu?"

The butcher pursed his lips and nodded with confidence. He said something quickly over his shoulder, and the man making the fire pit came over. He was younger than the butcher but older than Jacoby, dressed in all red - shirt, pants, clogs - and he was huge, towering over the tall butcher. The man in red had curt, sandy hair straight back off his remarkable face, handsome to the square inch and bulging with enthusiasm. Jacoby thought on the spot that he had discovered the face of Italy. The butcher introduced the man to him as his son, also a butcher. They shook, and Jacoby's hand disappeared into the massive mitt, pecked with scar tissue and hard as an ax handle, of the butcher's son.

The butcher said something to his son that Jacoby could not make out, but the reverential tone and the eyes on Jacoby as he spoke, plus the reference to "cinghiale," allowed Jacoby to infer that the father was telling the son about his slaying of the wild boar.

"Bravo," the son said in a marvelously deep voice.

"Grazie," Jacoby said and then asked his name. "Come ti chiami?"

"Dario," he responded and went back to building the fire pit.

"Guarda," the butcher asked Jacoby to look as he carefully pulled back the foil from the covered object on the table, revealing an enormous porchetta loin, sealed in golden pig skin and the aromatics evident at the end and also in the aroma that prompted Jacoby's appetite. "Un po' per colazione?" the butcher asked.

"Sì," Jacoby agreed as a little porchetta for breakfast sounded like the best idea imaginable at the moment.

The butcher went to the van and returned with a basket of rolls. He quickly separated one and then made thin slices from the end of the porchetta loin. Boy, who had been exploring the property, came bounding over to join.

"Un po' per lui?" Jacoby asked the butcher as the dog arrived whimpering.

"Certo," the butcher said and continued slicing. He piled half the pink meat, studded with garlic and rosemary and sage, on the roll and handed it to Jacoby. The rest he piled on a plastic plate and put it on the ground. Jacoby and Boy took to their breakfast with equal vigor. The flavor of the roasted meat was complimented perfectly by the aromatics, and the crisp, unctuous skin snapped and oozed its underbelly upon contact and covered everything in his mouth with silky, flavorful fat. The bread did a nice job of keeping it all together and absorbing the drippings. It also prevented the need for awkward cutlery, so the guests could eat standing, if they chose, or even sitting on the slope toward the villa.

"Incredibile," Jacoby told the butcher when he was able to speak. "Bravo."

The butcher nodded and held up a hand. He went to the van and pulled a white cooler close to the doorway. "Bistecce e salsicce," he said and pushed the cooler back into the shaded compartment.

"Perfetto," Jacoby said, comforted by the fact that no matter what else happened that day, all would eat well.

•   •   •

Giovanni and Nicoletta ferried wine bottles in a wheelbarrow from a far side of the consortium into the main production area. These were bottles from the previous harvests, properly aged, and newly labeled with the operation's first insignia, featuring the sketched cinghiale conceived and funded by Dolores, and marked by their proper designation of "Colli Fiorentini" indicating the hills of Florence. They set up the bottles on a makeshift bar among the chrome vats and oak barrels so the guests could see the wine making operation while also finding shade. The young couple, bartenders for the day, also filled metal tubs of icy water with bottles of prosecco and acqua minerale.

Jacoby, confident in all that he saw, and not wanting to appear scrutinous, took Boy for a walk around the perimeter of the property to rehearse the spiel he had for the journalists. The sun spread gently on his face as they toured the treeline that bordered the grounds beyond the villa. Boy dashed in and out of the woods, chasing scents or small creatures in the bramble. There were only streaks of clouds and a slight breeze that would likely drop as the temperature rose. The day could not have been more perfect, and Jacoby savored the contentment while breathing in the crisp air scented by the lush surroundings. He detected truffles in the area and thought, at some point, to train Boy to find them. A gust of wind set small leaves to clapping as Jacoby turned back toward the villa that was beautifully perched on a ridge with the hills beyond rolling into infinity. The far side of the house was obscured by scaffolding, and Jacoby imagined the work complete and the property open to visitors. Hints of dust arrived on the breeze, and Jacoby realized the first guests were agitating the dirt road with their arrival.

Before returning to the festival area, Jacoby stopped for a moment by the mausoleum behind the villa. He thought of Bill and wondered if Filippo rested for eternity inside the family tomb. Or if he was still alive. Consideration of this was interrupted by the honk of a car horn, and Jacoby watched a small parade of cars approach the parking area near the consortium. "Come on, Boy," Jacoby said and hurried down the slope to greet the first guests.

The first guests were groups of older villagers, and Jacoby was touched by their support and enthusiasm. They were dressed nicely and in great spirits, perhaps feeling some pride in the expansion of the local brand. Jacoby greeted each and directed all, as best he could in Italian, toward the food and drink. An expat journalist from California arrived on the back of her Italian boyfriend's Ducati, and Jacoby's day as an official host and salesman began.

By the time he had walked the journalist and her boyfriend around the consortium and up to the villa, Dolores had arrived in a leopard print minidress with matching mules. She brought a small entourage of her well-heeled Chiantishire girlfriends, all dressed to the nines and drinking prosecco in the sunlight. Paolo and his crew appeared from the far side of the consortium, carrying wicker baskets of freshly bottled oil. The old Italian men and the young British women immediately formed an incongruous gaggle punctuated by frequent peels of high-pitched laughter.

And then the party really started. Younger people from the village, Giovanni's peers, arrived en masse. A touring bus churned up the hill and parked on the lawn. Helen was the first one out, followed by a parade of journalists, all female, dressed like casual professionals, with their tools for reporting in fancy bags or backpacks. They wore a squad of hats and sunglasses and sensible yet stylish shoes. After the journalists all departed the bus, a dozen or so Jacoby tallied, three enormous men, including the driver, followed. The driver had a shaved head and tattoos on all parts of his skin below the neck not covered by clothes. A second man, almost as big as the first, had a long braided beard, a man-bun in back and a crazed look in his eyes. Jacoby recognized the last man - onyx and chiseled in a crisp, white dress shirt - as Rodrigue, the calcio storico player married to one of Helen's friends. Their arrival, as conjured by Helen for security and transportation purposes, brought tremendous relief to Jacoby at the affordable price of the bus rental plus all the three men could eat and drink, which looked like a lot, but still a bargain.

Jacoby hugged Helen as the three bruisers beelined for the food station manned by the butcher and his son, where smoke, smelling of steak and sausages, billowed from the makeshift grill. Bruna mingled with some older locals, while the younger contingency gathered around the bar manned by Giovanni and Nicoletta. The journalists poked around, smiling, taking pictures, chatting with each other. Dolores held court. Everyone was drinking; many were eating the porchetta sliders; the sun was shining. It was all going as planned, and Jacoby wished he and Helen, their arms around each other, could be captured in marble, like Daphne and Apollo, so that moment would last forever.

Chapter 41

The journalists raved about the property and expressed repeated astonishment at the location's undiscovered status. They took pictures and asked many questions. Jacoby knew how writer's loved to come across hidden gems, and he sensed their churning competitiveness as they toured the grounds with their wheels spinning the story in their heads. He imagined the positive press would come very soon. The wine and olive oil also impressed, and Jacoby arranged for a bottle of each to go home with the journalists.

The butcher's son turned out to be an aficionado of Dante's *Divine Comedy*, and everyone gathered around when he stepped on top of the cooler and began reciting passages with great physical animation in his bellowing voice. Helen sidled up to Jacoby, took his hand and whispered in his ear, "Only in Italy would a butcher have a love of poetry." Jacoby smiled and thought throughout the performance, not understanding the language at all, of the quote from Dante he learned from his father and shared often with Bill, about fate being a gift that could not be taken from us. And then Jacoby's phone vibrated in his pocket. It was Bill.

Jacoby swiveled through the crowd and away from the gathering toward the entrance to the property. "Pronto? Pronto?" he said into the phone. "Bill? Bill? You there?"

There was no connection, and Jacoby raised his thumb to return the call, but he stopped at the sound of an engine roar and the sight of

Boy running frantically from the woods in his direction. The hunter's jeep, in a cloud of dust, appeared from the tree cover and hurtled toward the gathering. Jacoby watched it approach as Boy settled beside him, breathing heavily and shaking. The phone in Jacoby's hand shuddered, indicating a voicemail, but he put it in his pocket as the jeep, full of men with the hunter behind the wheel, sped directly toward him and then skidded to a stop, sliding across the grass at an abrupt angle. Jacoby could feel the crowd appear behind him, but he kept his eyes on the hunter who approached, disheveled and possibly drunk, with four men at his back.

"Who in the good fuck is this?" Dolores asked.

The hunter didn't slow down when approaching, and Jacoby waited until he could smell the grappa before he punched the hunter in the mouth, knocking him to the ground. Someone screamed. Boy began barking. Jacoby's hand throbbed. The hunter's men pounced on Jacoby with punches and kicks, and he curled into a ball on the ground and protected his head and privates. Before any real damage could be done, he heard raised voices of men and felt the attack diminish. When he opened his eyes, the hunter and his friends were being pummeled by Rodrigue and his teammates. The butcher's son had one of the hunter's off the ground by his shirt, shaking him like a rag doll.

Helen helped Jacoby up and inspected his face. "My god," she gasped. "Are you alright?"

Jacoby brushed off his clothes and only felt slight damage to his torso. "Yeah," he said. "Good call on the security."

Jacoby crept up to the melee, watched the hunter and his friends get beaten for a moment and then yelled, "Basta."

His declaration of "enough" was heard. The calciante stopped kicking the crap out of their overmatched opponents. The butcher's son dropped the shaken man to the ground. Jacoby stood over the hunter, who lay in a fetal position on the ground, bleeding from above his eye and cradling his ribs. Jacoby tapped his side three times, and Boy adhered to the command and arrived next to his master. "Sit," Jacoby ordered; the dog obeyed.

Jacoby got the hunter's attention by chucking the fallen man's chin with the tip of his shoe. "Ascolta," he told him to listen. "Questo è mio cane. Capito?"

The hunter did not answer, and the crowd at Jacoby's back, including his enforcers, crept closer. The hunter sensed their energy and skirted a few feet away on his haunches. He slowly got to his feet and checked his jaw for fracture and wiped away some blood on his face with a sleeve. His men struggled to their feet, the fight gone from their eyes.

"Capito?" Jacoby asked again if the hunter recognized the dog as his.

The hunter looked over the crowd that opposed him, staring a moment at his wife who held the arm of Giovanni. He turned his eyes to Jacoby and nodded.

"Vai," Jacoby told him to go.

The defeated men hobbled into the jeep and drove away from the property. All who remained watched in silence until someone yelled, "Jake! Il americano!" The crowd erupted in cheers and Rodrigue lifted Jacoby's hand in the air to declare victory. Jake nodded in appreciation and gave the beautiful man a giant hug.

The party resumed with a new fervor, and everyone shared in the spirit of having witnessed something totally unexpected, frightening, and exhilarating in the aftermath. Wine was poured and food consumed. Jacoby made the rounds and functioned as host in a new light, feeling so relieved and uplifted that he forgot all about the voicemail from Bill.

Chapter 42

The party eventually, as planned, moved from the estate to the village piazza with the tattooed bus driver ferrying all the guests who had come from the city along with many of the workers on the property who were invited to join the festivities. Villagers who had not attended the festival came to the piazza, and by sundown, the square hosted a bustling party. The butcher and his son opened up the shop and layered the display counter with meats and cheeses and the remaining porchetta. Bottles of wine, brought back from the estate, were opened and poured. Children crowded around the calciante, asking questions and shadow boxing. Giovanni hopped on the precipice of the statue and sang an aria from *Rigoletto*. Jacoby brought the journalists into the hotel and poured them glasses of Brunello di Montalcino from his collection behind the bar.

By the time night settled and the party goers gathered to go home, Jacoby was exhausted. He saw everyone off from the piazza with proper grace and appreciation and then went into the hotel with Helen and Boy. They settled on the couch in the front room, and Helen rested her head on Jacoby's shoulder. He fell asleep. It was a heavy sleep, and dreams came fast. He saw the man again in Rome, and the bruzzico on the horizon at dawn. He woke up instantly. "Holy shit," he yelped, rousing Helen.

"What is it?" she asked, clutching his forearm.

"Bill," he said. "Bill called."

"When?"

"Earlier, just as the hunter and them were pulling up."

"Well," she said. "Call him back!"

Jacoby rose quickly from the couch and found his phone on the front desk in the lobby. Helen followed him out and stood by his side as he accessed the voicemail with a shaky hand. Jacoby's teeth chattered as he waited for the message to play.

"Put in on speaker, for god's sake," Helen implored.

He put it on speaker and did not breath until Bill's voice emerged:

Hello, Jacoby. Please forgive my absence, but the most fantastic thing has happened. Filippo is indeed alive, and we are together in Abruzzo. There is so much to explain and consider, not the least of which is that you have a living relative who you must meet immediately. We will return to Rome tomorrow morning, and I would like you to join us there. I also feel that it would be wonderful if Helen were able to accompany you, so please bring her along. You will understand when you get here. Ta.

The line went dead. Jacoby and Helen exchanged dumbfounded looks until she smacked him hard across the shoulder. "Oh my god!" she screamed. "Is this actually happening?"

Jacoby shook his head and rubbed his shoulder. He felt faint yet also electric, as if fate was somehow being delivered once again.

• • •

Helen went home to Florence by taxi after hearing the voice message from Bill. She could accompany Jacoby to Rome but had to pack. She would meet Jacoby at Santa Maria Novella the next morning. Jacoby remained at the hotel and barely slept, his heart and thoughts racing throughout the night, yet he was up and alert and out the door at the break of dawn. He left Boy with Nicoletta, and after a quick caffè, he called a cab. Jacoby watched the Bruzzico through the window as the car snaked along the ridge road before descending into Florence proper.

At the station, he bought two business class tickets and waited for Helen. She arrived promptly at 7:00, dressed in a pleated, plaid skirt with a matching jacket over a white blouse. Jacoby also looked sharp, in a hand-tailored Italian shirt of blue and white checks complimented by slate, wool slacks. They both wore Italian shoes and had overnight bags, though it was unclear how many nights they would be staying over. The couple met with nervous smiles and boarded the train without speaking.

The situation could not be discussed, and Jacoby took great satisfaction in knowing that he and Helen could be silent around each other. He took her hand and kissed her on the forehead; she touched his cheek and smiled with all of her warmth and beauty. The train rumbled from the station, and Jacoby's chin dropped to his chest. He was fast asleep before they passed beyond the ramparts of the city.

He woke up a half-hour from Rome. Helen put away her phone and motioned toward the cornetto and caffè she had put on the serving tray in front of him. "Thanks," he said with a scratchy voice.

"Do you know where we're meeting up with them?" Helen asked.

"I assume the apartment where Bill and I have been staying by Campo de' Fiori."

Helen clapped twice quickly. "In all of the excitement, I forgot how much I love Rome," she said. "Let's stay a few days?"

"OK," Jacoby said as he pulled the cornetto into strips and let them dissolve in his mouth and stared out the window.

He continued to stare until the train began to warble upon entry into Rome. Nerves began to rise in Jacoby once they entered the dark tunnels that fed into the station. He'd been fixated on Bill's situation and not recognizing that he was about to meet what was most likely the only living relative he had on earth, who just happened to be the lover of his closest friend. "This is so crazy," he turned to Helen to say.

"I know!" she beamed. "I'm so excited for all of you. So much has happened, and I feel so lucky to be a witness."

"I love you," Jacoby said to Helen for the first time.

Her head and neck lunged back as a soft smile spread across her mouth. "Thank you," she said. "And I love you, as well."

They kissed on the lips, and Helen began to giggle. "What?" Jacoby asked with a curious smile.

"Go brush your teeth, lover," she said. "Can't meet your long lost uncle with dragon breath."

Jacoby laughed and went off to the bathroom with his toiletry bag. When he returned, the train was making its last lurches toward the platform. Jacoby and Helen grabbed their belongings and waited by the door. They were the first ones off the train, and they bound along the nearly empty platform and through the station busy with morning commuters. They waited in the morning sun for a cab and climbed into a shining sedan.

"Buongiorno," Jacoby said to the driver. "Campo de' Fiore, per favore."

Chapter 43

Jacoby tried to distract himself on the cab ride by pointing out the landmarks of which he had recently become familiar. Helen patted him on the leg and said, "I've been here before, you know?"

"You have?" he feigned ignorance.

"Once or twice," she said and kept her hand on his thigh as they rode the rest of the way in silence.

Near the Campo, Jacoby paid the driver and held Helen's hand as she stepped onto the shifted cobblestones. They threw their bags over their shoulders and walked down the shaded lane that fed into the piazza. The morning was cool and bright, a hint of chill in the air. Jacoby focused on his breath, taking it in and out through his nose. He wondered what Filippo would be like as he admired the pastel facades of the noble buildings complemented by the floral abundance of Rome. Helen walked with enthusiasm beside him, practically bouncing. He was so glad she had come along.

They came upon the door to the apartment building, and Jacoby paused. "Come here," he said impulsively and took Helen by the hand. "I have to show you something first."

They entered through the low archway into the secret courtyard. Jacoby skidded to a stop. Bill was there, by the fountain with an elegant, slender man of tawny complexion and dark hair combed straight back off his wrinkled forehead, his hands in the pockets of designer pants.

"Hello, Jacoby. Hello, Helen, " Bill said as if expecting them. "We are so glad you have arrived."

Jacoby approached them, staring at his great uncle who smiled with enormous warmth. "Ciao, Giacomo," he said.

Puzzled and mesmerized, Jacoby continued and stuck out his hand, out of habit, for a shake. The elegant man, his great uncle, threw out his arms and kissed Jacoby with red lips on both cheeks. He then held Jacoby by the shoulders and looked him over carefully.

"Sì. Sì," he said. "You are a Zanobini. È vero."

Jacoby flushed with pride and wonder. This man was his family. They were aligned in height and appearance. No wonder Bill took to Jacoby like he did. Happy spiders crawled all over Jacoby's body, and he felt deliverance and redemption and the awe of being alive.

"I know this is all very much, Jacoby," Bill said gently, from a considered distance away. "But there's more. Things I did not know myself until yesterday."

Jacoby stared at his uncle, studying familiar features and feeling the same blood course through the both of them. Even distracted, Jacoby had heard Bill's words and knew them to be true. He turned to his friend. "What more?" he asked. "Why did he call me Giacamo?"

Bill looked at Jacoby with overwhelming compassion until his eyes turned abruptly away toward the borders of the courtyard.

"Because that is the name I gave you," a woman's voice said from the direction in which Bill stared.

Jacoby turned to find a woman beyond a small staircase. She stood in a doorway crying, a shaking hand over her mouth. Jacoby recognized her instantly, from his memories, her dark hair and beauty, and the matter of his being poured out of him like a loaded barrel severed at its base. He smelled cookies being baked. Helen burst out crying.

"What?" Jacoby asked as emotion rushed his nose, filled his chest and teared his eyes. "What?"

Bill came over and put his hand on Jacoby's forearm. He began to speak in a kind voice to Jacoby who did not take his eyes from the woman in the threshold. His mother. His mother. Chills permeated every pore and cell of his body. He broke from Bill's grip and approached her, unable to feel his feet as he walked. He stopped at the bottom of the staircase. The engraving over the door read "Bruzzico."

"Mommy," he said, almost within reach of her embrace.

She reached out her hands and then put them down. "Mamma," she corrected and raised her arms again to give her son the hug he had longed for ever since he was a little boy.

The End

About the Author

Andrew Cotto is the award-winning author of five novels and a regular contributor to the *New York Times*. Andrew has also written for *Parade, Men's Journal, Rolling Stone, La Cucina Italiana, Condé Nast Traveler, Rachael Ray In Season, Italy magazine, Maxim, AARP* and more. He lives in Brooklyn, New York.

Acknowledgments

Thanks to all who shared the passions depicted in *Cucina Tipica* and inspired, as a result, this sequel. I've made so many Italophile friends along the way, and my life is richer as a result.

Thank you to Virginia Valenzuela for the line edits, and special thanks to Carlos Dews for correcting my awful Italian. Finally, thanks to Black Rose Writing for the continued support in publishing.

Note from the Author

Word-of-mouth is crucial for any author to succeed. If you enjoyed *Cucina Romana*, please leave a review online—anywhere you are able. Even if it's just a sentence or two. It would make all the difference and would be very much appreciated.

Thanks!
Andrew Cotto

Thank you so much for reading one of Andrew Cotto's novels.

If you enjoyed our book, please check out our recommendation for your next great read!

Cucina Tipica by Andrew Cotto

"Whether you love Italy, dream of visiting it one day (like myself) or just want to enjoy an incredibly enjoyable book set in a beautiful part of the world, I thoroughly recommend this story as the best I have ever read!"

–*Midwest Book Review*

View other Black Rose Writing titles at www.blackrosewriting.com/books and use promo code **PRINT** to receive a **20% discount** when purchasing.

Made in United States
North Haven, CT
07 June 2022

19962250R00129